D0041704

S I N G L E T U S K

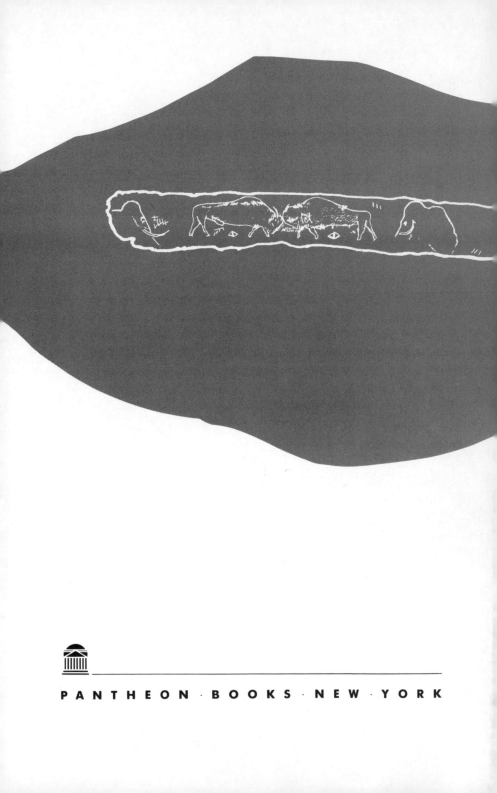

PANTHEON · BOOKS · NEW · YORK

SINGLETUSK

BJÖRN KURTÉN

A · NOVEL · OF · THE · ICE · AGE

Library of Congress
Cataloging-in-Publication Data

Kurtén, Björn.
Singletusk.

Sequel to: Dance of the tiger.
I. Title.
PT9876.21.U7S5   1986
839.7'374   85-43460
ISBN 0-394-55352-7

Design by Guenet Abraham

Manufactured in the United States of America

CONTENTS

ACKNOWLEDGMENTS

I am grateful to friends and colleagues for discussion and advice: Elaine Anderson, Joakim Donner, Mikael Fortelius, the late John E. Guilday, R. Dale Guthrie, Åke Hultkrantz, Carl-Axel Moberg, Göran Sandell, and many others. Margaret Newman's graphic description of an encounter in Africa gave me the idea for the initial scene in the "Harrier" chapter. The late Hubert Pepper contributed ideas on the art of the Ice Age, and also a number of maxims (Pepper's Paleolithic Proverbs). My wife and children have been a constant support during these years, and I dedicate the book to them.

Björn Kurtén

June 1979–March 1984

INTRODUCTION

S i n g l e t u s k is the sequel to *Dance of the Tiger,* a novel which carried the reader back into life 30,000 years ago, when two completely different species of human beings co-existed. It was the story of a dramatic encounter between the two peoples—the courtly, blond, matriarchal Neandertals (called the Whites) and the aggressive, swarthy, patriarchal *Homo sapiens* (called the Blacks). Above all, it was the story of Tiger, son of the chief of a peaceful village of *Homo sapiens* hunters, and of his passion to avenge his people. The only survivor of a savage attack against his tribe, Tiger roamed the landscapes of Ice Age Europe, hunting mammoth and saber-tooth tiger, braving a world of constant danger, and always searching for Shelk, the brutal warrior who had killed his father.

Completely alone and badly wounded, Tiger was rescued by a clan of Neandertals—the alien creatures he had heard about but never seen. On the clan's island, far in the north, Tiger learned the Neandertal language, fell in love with Veyde, their proud and beautiful leader, and discovered the deeply human side of a people he had despised as barbaric. And, finally, Tiger came face to face with Shelk in a confrontation that called up all the cunning for which he was named. By the time the story ended, the reader had discovered what may be the solution to prehistory's most puzzling mystery —the disappearance of the Neandertals from the face of the earth.

Singletusk begins a generation after *Dance of the Tiger*. Those who were young then appear now as the parent generation. Tiger, the Black man, and his White woman, Veyde, live with her clan on their island surrounded by their children, who are Brown (hybrids) and sterile. Then there is Tiger's half-brother, Baywillow, who is also one of the Browns (a hybrid) and his (actually, Tiger's) children by a Black woman, Hind. The older generation from *Dance of the Tiger* lives in their memories as half-mythical beings. What endures is the contrast between the highly ritualized and matriarchal White society and that of the patriarchal Blacks; the prodigious animal life of the Ice Age; and the compact between man and the Powers—a Sun God, animal Guardians, and spirits.

According to the custom of the Whites, a childless man would ask his brother to impregnate his woman, and so Baywillow's children are in fact Tiger's. As a result, the family ties on Veyde's Island are somewhat chaotic, jet-set fashion, and the reader may find the accompanying genealogical table (see page xi) useful. Note that the Blacks have names from the animal kingdom and the Whites names from the plant kingdom. For the hybrid Browns the White system is followed, with the exception of Tiger's son Marten and the legendary Shelk of *Dance of the Tiger*.

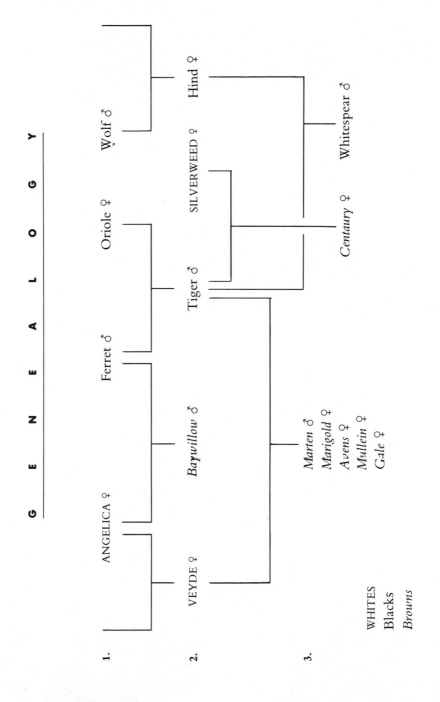

GENEALOGY

1.

ANGELICA ♀   Barwillow ♂   Ferret ♂   Oriole ♀   Wolf ♂

2.

VEYDE ♀   Tiger ♂   SILVERWEED ♀   Hind ♀

Centaury ♀   Whitespear ♂

3.

Marten ♂
Marigold ♀
Avens ♀
Mullein ♀
Gale ♀

WHITES
Blacks
Browns

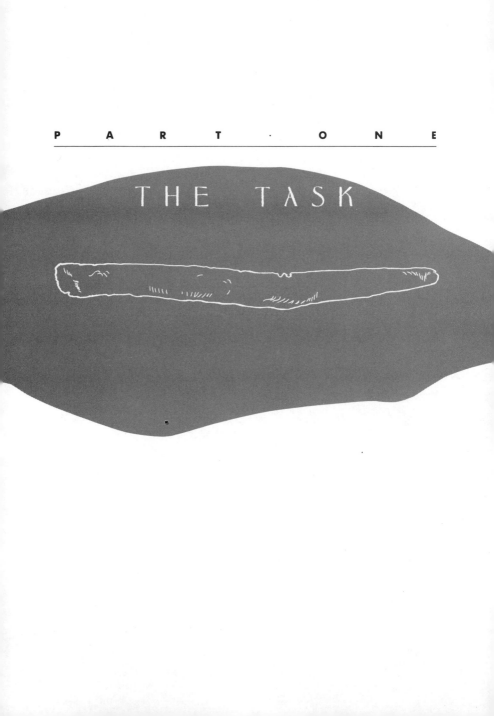

PART ONE

THE TASK

THE · GUARDIANS

On c e , w h e n he was still a small boy, his mother showed him the Guardians.

She was a Black woman, and she was called Hind. Slim and youthful, she seemed to him incredibly beautiful compared with the thickset, short-legged White women of their island tribe. She had black hair and dark eyes, and her complexion was a soft brown like the bark of a young pine tree. To him she was invariably kind, though with others she could be uncertain in her moods. What he remembered best, because of its ending, was that raspberry-picking ramble on Veyde's Island.

It was an afternoon in late summer. Mother and son spoke as always in the quick, flexible tongue of the Blacks; in all those summers and winters, she had never bothered to learn to speak White. He walked slowly, with bent back and dragging steps, for he was pretending to be old Silverbirch the healer looking for plantain, and Silverbirch was so ancient and doddery he could hardly walk. Hind chided him gently for making fun of the old man, who had endeared himself to her by being able to speak Black after a fashion.

When they came to the raspberries, he forgot all about being a great healer. The tall plants formed a jungle in which the berries glowed magically. Everywhere there was a gleam of gossamer. The big spiders patrolled their webs assiduously, but scuttled quickly away when he loomed up. A clegg alighted on his hand, too sluggish even to bite, and he blew it away lightly, not wanting to crush it. Farther on, the raspberries gave way to meadowsweet, among which were the pods of red campion like small bags filled with seeds. Now the boy and his mother approached the long moraine point of the island, thrusting into the sea in a swirl of breakers under the strong wind. Yellow tansy flamed around them, big and bulbous like outsize mayweed flowers stripped of their white petals.

Massed clouds swept by, their outlines changing at every moment. Oh, they were the Guardians, rushing past to gather for some tremendous confabulation, gesticulating excitedly yet inscrutably to each other in their haste. They would take any number of shapes, but if you looked closely you could glimpse, now and then, their true form and that of their flock. There was He of the Bison, He of the Lion, He of the Horse, moving high above the heads of men. Yet that they chose to reveal themselves at all, even to a small boy like himself, was reassuring. They cared. They would not forget that men depended upon them. To them you prayed before the hunt, and to them you offered your thanks after its completion.

Of all the Powers, the Guardians were those that meant most to man. They were the rightful owners of the game. Of course, the spirits were close to man, too, in a way: each tree, each rock, each blade of grass had its spirit. Some spirits were great, like that of the sea; others were small, like that of a stone. But they didn't concern themselves much with men, and if you broke a branch, you could appease the spirit of the tree with a murmur of excuse.

Then there were other, mightier Powers whom no one knew much about. They were even greater than the Guardians, and ordinary people had little to do with them. The healers of the Whites and the shamans of the Blacks had some knowledge of these Powers. They decreed the fates of men, and you did better not to think much about them. The Guardians were a very different matter.

Presently they were gone. Shining in the afternoon sunlight, a thunderhead rose to awesome height. Its flat top drew out into ears, and the boy recognized the shape even before Hind told him. He was in the presence of the Guardian of the mammoth, the greatest of them all. You did not use the name of the mammoth freely if you were Black, though you could swear by it. Otherwise you called him the White Spears, for his tusks, or Twotails, or the Black Hill, or the Thunderer. And the boy felt his heart beating strongly within him, for his own name was Whitespear.

AVENS

The island shore was a confusion of boulders large and small, black, white, and red, some rooted firmly in the ground, others wobbling underfoot. The sea was a mirror where the islands in their summer glory seemed to float upon their own perfect reflections, as if swimming in a void. Distant isles and rocks hovered well above the edge of the world. Not a breath of wind was felt on that day of summer solstice.

Two young people walked along the beach, picking their way from one boulder to the next, unconsciously testing the foothold at each step: a girl and, behind her, a boy. Both carried packs on their backs and short javelins in their hands. The girl was talking in a persuasive, singsong flow, casting occasional glances over her shoulder. The boy listened attentively, nodding now and then.

He was a tall young man, still beardless, with brown skin,
very dark eyes, and wavy black hair. His clothing, in the
heat of high summer, consisted of a simple and rather tat-
tered loincloth made from marten skin, brown with white
patches. The girl, almost as tall as he, had a lighter complexion and chestnut hair. She was broader of face, with a snub
nose, but her proud brown eyes beneath commanding brows
and the fine curve of her wide mouth added up to beauty.
Her clothing was even scantier than his, merely tassels of
deerskin hanging from a belt.

The boy's gaze, fixed on her slim back, held nothing but
anxious concentration. She was holding forth; he was trying
to follow her.

The boy's real name was a secret, if an open one, and he
was called Whitespear. The girl's was no secret: it was
Avens. Yet she too had a secret name, one with immense
significance in the belief of her people, and nobody would
speak it except in a time of dire need.

Suddenly something flashed past their eyes with a great
whir and thudded down on the ground before their feet,
writhing, fighting, crawling. The boy ducked and jumped
back involuntarily. The girl, breaking off her harangue,
lifted her javelin with a curiously masculine gesture and bent
down to look.

It was two great dragonflies, locked in a death grip. The
one on top was speckled black and green, the other was
brown. Their wings, like blades of thin ice, whirred in a
frenzy, but otherwise the fight was silent. The girl went
down on her knees, her face alight with interest.

"Like eats like, Whitespear," she said. "Look!"

The green-and-black dragonfly had caught the other from
above. Its odd, platelike jaws were working deep in the back
of its prey. The brown dragonfly crawled wildly about on
the lichen-covered rock, carrying its inexorable attacker with
it. To the boy, who had bent down to peer at closer range,
the sight was gruesome because of the utter outlandishness

of the creatures. He had never looked closely at a dragonfly before. There was no fur, no warmth, no voice to proclaim their suffering, no breath to be stilled in death, only that incessant rustling of icy wings. There was not even a pair of eyes to read a soul into. These were not human, not animal, but creatures out of a nightmare, fighting things hewn out of rock and ice. He thought briefly of the pike he had caught earlier that day, of its firmly muscled body alive in his hands, its hungry living eyes meeting his own with the green darkness of the sea looking out of them. With that magnificent fish fighting in his grip he had felt a surge of brotherhood. These things were alien. He stepped back in disgust.

The green-and-black dragonfly had detached one wing of its prey, and it lay glittering among the bright yellow lichenroses. The maimed creature was struggling to get away from its attacker.

"It's filthy!" the boy cried. "I'll kill them!"

The girl held him back. "Don't, Whitespear. I want to watch. Do you see? He's bitten off the second wing."

"I don't want to see them! They look horrible. Not like animals at all. Not like anything."

"He's eaten off almost half of its back now. By the Mammoth, Whitespear! I didn't know you were so squeamish."

"Well, it isn't right." The boy tried to explain: "Like shouldn't eat like. It's wrong. Did you ever see hyena eating hyena, Avens?"

The girl pondered this for a moment. Then she shook her head.

"There you are. Not even hyenas—and they'll eat anything! But dragonflies—and I've always thought them beautiful—"

"They *are* beautiful," said Avens firmly. "The dragonfly is *my* bird. This green-and-black one, of course. He's winning. I saw him being born. He crept out of his old skin and sat quite still, and the wings grew out on his back while the sun moved across the sky."

Whitespear sat down on a boulder and looked at her. Then he started to laugh softly. Avens took no notice; she was watching the end of the fight. "I have looked at dragonflies many times," she murmured. "Now I know which one it is —my bird. I know something else, too. Their wings are *not* made of thin ice—the ice you get on the rock pools after the first frost. I shall have wings like that someday. But I'll still be able to speak." She rose serenely. "It's over. We must go, Whitespear. Marigold will be waiting for you."

"And for that pike I got," said the boy, still smiling. "Avens, sometimes I can't make you out."

"Why?" said Avens, surprised. "I tell you all my thoughts." She picked up her javelin and started to walk away, holding herself very erect, as if balancing an eider egg on her head. There was a light of demure pleasure in her eyes. Whitespear shrugged his shoulders and followed her.

.   .   .

"And that," said Whitespear, "was the First Sign."

He was telling his story many years later, in a very different world. Lying in a tent, he looked out at an ice-bound tarn, dazzlingly white under the winter sun. The great forest was massed around the lake, the pines grey and white with frost. From time to time, there was a slight rustling as a pile of snow detached itself from a pine-crown and slid down through the branches, and once the distant *clong* of a raven was heard. Otherwise, the only sound was that of Whitespear's voice, and an occasional murmured answer from the girl who listened to him. She was on her knees, holding his hand, her face bent over his.

"So you say your name is Oriole?" He looked down at her, smiled, and went on:

"Do you know the oriole? A bird of tales and dreams, you say? Taking the shape of every bird under the sun, but always yellow, bright yellow like the sun itself. Yes. But listen to me.

"She is real. As real as the wagtail who went tip-tap-toe when I left the islands, with his eye upon me, and saying *slee-slee,* wary as always.

"She is real, I tell you. But she lives far away to the south, and the Blacks, our people, brought her name with them from where they came: from the Land of Flints and still farther away. So Avens told me, she who was my friend, and she knew most things. Among the Whites the tales live forever, but among us Blacks they fade out and only the names remain. So listen to me, for my story should live.

"To the Whites, the oriole is the Sunbird. To me, she is the bird of my soul. I have three names, and two of them are White: Vetch and Sunbird. Vetch is the name given me by my father Baywillow, and the Sunbird goes with it, for every plant on the earth has its bird in the sky. I think now that you, Oriole, were sent to me by a benign Power, and I am right thankful.

"I am known by my Black name, which is Whitespear. That's a riddle too, but one you know. Yes, of course, no one in his senses would give a small boy the real name of that creature. Yet my mother Hind had dreams night after night before I was born, and the Powers spoke to her in mammoth shape.

"There is more behind it. I know now that my father Baywillow was doomed to be childless like all of his kin. Avens knew—she knew almost everything—and she told me. I, like my brothers and sisters, all gone now, was sired by Tiger, my father's brother. You know the bond that exists between the black tiger and the mammoth. Once Tiger told me about the spirit of his childhood lake: it partook of tiger and of mammoth in its upper and its nether shape. I asked him to make a picture, but he didn't want to. There are things too great and powerful to be rendered. Still, he too had dreams. So I am Whitespear.

"Now I must tell you of Avens and her family. We were born on the same day, Avens and I, but to different mothers. My mother Hind was Black. Avens's mother was Veyde, a White woman, and Tiger, a Black man, was her father. Avens was the third in that brood. In the end they were five, always born three summers apart. The eldest was Marten, and he was the only one with a Black name. The others were all girls, and they had flower names, White fashion: Marigold, Avens, Mullein, Gale. After that, Veyde was barren.

"They lived, all of them: nothing could harm them. The ague took my brother. It wanted Marten too, and he sank into it as you sink into the sea. He was gone but he came back, rose up, and was well. The adder killed my sister as she climbed a tree; it was up on a branch and struck her in the groin. Gale, too, was stung by an adder. Her foot swelled up and turned green and blue. She hid in the woods, and came back healed.

"They were very different from one another, those five, but in one thing they were the same. Before my soul's eye they seemed larger than other people. Not as to height— they were no taller than us Blacks, though the girls were taller than you, Oriole. In other ways, though, and each of them in a different way, they were children of the Gods, and that's what the Whites called them.

"Take Marten. He was tall and straight like a spear. There never was a better hunter on Veyde's Island, and he was the pride of his father. He feared nothing and nobody, and he was stronger than anybody else. I saw him kill a bear with a single thrust of his spear. And his eyes! I tell you he had the eyes of a kite under the sun and of an owl under the stars. I remember standing with him on the beach, and him pointing to the reeds at the other side of the bay and saying that he could see the young of the sandpiper there, running about like voles. I couldn't see them.

"Marten's eyes were large and brown under the heavy brow of the Whites, just like his sisters'. Your eyes, Oriole, are black like mine. The eyes of the Whites are light—they shine blue or green, like ice.

"Most of all, though, I admired Marten's keenness of hearing. You know the courtship dance of the capercaillie. It snaps its beak with a click, and we can hear that; but it whistles, too, and only Marten heard that. Once we heard a seagull calling in the fog. Marten listened and said, 'It's going away.' A little later he said, 'Now it's coming this way.' Sure enough, a few breaths later it passed just over our heads. He told me it raises the pitch of its cry when it's coming towards you. Oh yes. The footfall of the lynx is as silent as the fall of a snowflake, but he heard it.

"Marigold was very different. She was named for the great yellow marsh marigold that blooms along the streams and ditches in early spring, and indeed, she too was large and beautiful. She was tall and fat, and as lazy as a clegg. She exuded a scent of sex day and night, summer and winter. From my thirteenth summer she rode me, and found joy in it. Oh, she was a glutton for anything that could be felt, eaten, smelled, tasted, or seen. She took everything to herself as if she were living the lives of a thousand people at once. I remember her rolling in the morning dew on the shore meadow, slowly and solemnly, with her arms stretched above her head. When the first snow came, she would stand with her mouth open and her eyes shut, catching the flakes on her tongue. She licked her body like a lynx.

"Oh, she was a witch! She loved to give you a scare. A snow-cold hand out of the dark, the hiss of an adder behind a rock—that was Marigold. Then she'd laugh and hug you. If she was a witch, at least she was a good-natured one."

.   .   .

Avens and Whitespear continued their walk, cutting through an alder thicket, wading across a narrow channel, and emerging on Veyde's Island. Both were silent. The boy,

usually taciturn, was feeling self-conscious about his outburst, while the girl, for the moment, had suspended her
habit of thinking out loud for his edification. Still, the walk
was lively enough. Indignant terns screeched and made
threatening dives at them as they passed through the nesting
territories. When one tern left off, satisfied with driving
away the intruders, the next would be galvanized into action.
Finally, as they came up on the shore meadow of Veyde's
Island, two equally indignant redshanks took wing and cir-
cled about, whistling mournfully, until the forest closed
about the invaders.

They were now making their way through the woods,
scrambling across moss-covered hogbacks and skirting bogs
where the last flyblown cloudberry blooms still shone white.
The air was heavy with the scent of labrador tea, and the
strident chorus of chaffinches echoed around them, each bird
repeating the trill of its neighbor in a fierce ecstasy of rivalry.
They passed a silent dark tarn under a grey cliff, where the
bogbean's cloverlike leaves swished about their feet, and
Whitespear smiled at a memory. As a child, he had been very
much afraid of the tarn; somebody, maybe Marigold, had
told him it was bottomless. He had told Avens, and she had
walked straight there and splashed across without getting
wet above her knees.

Presently, they stepped into a glade with isolated pine
trees. There was a figure crouched in the middle.

"Oh!" exclaimed Avens. "She's been taking bogbean soup
again. Marigold, I believe you do this for fun!"

The squatting girl raised a tear-stained face to them. When
she caught sight of Whitespear, a great relief seemed to flood
her features.

"So there you are," she said in an accusing voice. "About
time, too! You put them into me and then you go away."

"Don't be a fool," said Avens sharply. "I've had them too,
and Whitespear never even touched me, nor did anybody
else."

"Well, now you're here you can at least help me." Marigold's hands were fluttering anxiously. Whitespear obediently stepped behind her, squatted on his haunches, and
started to pull out the great slithery thing protruding between her ample buttocks. He hauled on it as on a rope,
Avens looking on critically.

Meanwhile, several other people had congregated about
them. They were clearly impressed but also highly enter-
tained by the spectacle. However, they remained politely
silent until the appearance of a large White woman, who
immediately doubled up with laughter. At that, eyes started
to wander and mouths to twitch. Somewhere there was a
deprecating click of a tongue, but it was too late. First one,
then several others, put their hands over their mouths and
fled. Choked sniggers could be heard through the insistent
noise of the chaffinches, and a great black-winged gull
swooping overhead gave a sudden throaty neigh as if
amused. Avens looked up. "He can see it," she said. "He'll
have it for dinner."

"Oh, you're a beast," panted Marigold, straining heavily.

"There isn't any end to it," murmured Whitespear. "It's
still as thick as ever." He went on hauling, hand over hand.

"Mother!" said Marigold. "You should not laugh. It is
not nice." She had spoken in the White language. Her
mother, trying to look contrite, answered, "I am sorry, Miss
Marigold, I truly am. Mister Whitespear, step aside, please.
I can handle it."

"It is almost out now, Miss Veyde," said Whitespear. "It
is getting thinner. Here we go, Miss Marigold. Did it hurt?"

Marigold rose and looked with some surprise at the great
glistening mass of tapeworm. "Not really, Mister Whitespear," she said graciously. "Not coming out, I mean. Before that, it gave me *such* a pa-a-ain—here!" She pointed
dramatically to her left breast, and Avens snorted impa-
tiently.

"My dear girl," said Veyde, hugging her solicitously. "I am sure it hurt terribly. It is all over now. There, there."

Avens turned a disdainful shoulder on her suffering sister and stared at the incredible coils of tapeworm with new interest. "I do believe this is the biggest you ever made, Miss Marigold," she said. She suddenly caught up the thin end of the worm in her hands and started to walk across the glade, so that the huge worm straightened out behind her. Occasionally, she looked back to see if it was all straight, but she had nearly reached the edge of the wood before the fat end began to move. Whitespear looked after her, frowning deeply as he tried to understand what she was doing. Avens began to step back, counting on her fingers as she did so.

"Six hands and a finger," she announced when she reached the others. "Lie down, Miss Marigold, please."

The order was given with such quiet authority that Marigold, to her own great surprise, lay down without a word of protest. Avens quickly stepped her length. "Three steps," she said. "You are a marvel, Miss Marigold."

Marigold sat up, outraged. "Of all things! Miss Avens, the Guardian of the hyena has touched your head."

"Now, now," Veyde interposed. "Such language! I am sure you are still dizzy, Miss Marigold. Come, we shall give you something nice to eat. You need it, after those horrible bogbeans."

"I have a pike for you," said Whitespear.

Marigold smiled. Then she said, with a catch in her voice, "I can only breed tapeworms. Other women breed babies."

Avens hesitated, then said curtly, "You are not the only one." She turned vehemently and strode off.

.   .   .

"Most Blacks think the Whites have no speech at all but jabber like small children—bah, bah, bah. And yet, my Oriole, my Sunbird, they do speak, but quite different from us. Yes, we Blacks speak in different tongues too. You hear a man talk and you say, He comes from the Salt Sea, or, He's from the Land of Flints. Yet you know what he's saying. It's the same with the chaffinch. I've heard the chaffinch in the North and in the South, and they do not sing quite the same, yet they are all chaffinches, even though some of them leave out that curly trill at the end of the song. And so it is with the tongue of the Blacks.

"That of the Whites is so different—different in every way. We at Veyde's Island spoke both tongues. At least we Blacks did. The Whites never learned to speak Black properly—maybe their tongues were too stiff. And Hind, my mother, didn't speak White. I wouldn't have thought much about this, but Avens did, and she often talked about it.

"She always wanted to know *why*. Why, she asked, do the Whites and the Blacks speak in different tongues? Why do the Whites call each other Miss and Mister and keep on saying Excuse me and Forgive me and Please and so on, when we don't? Why do the Whites cover their eyes with their hands in greeting, when we bow? Why are all their riddles and stories different from ours? Why do the Whites and the Blacks sing in such different ways? Why are the White names flower names and the Black names animal names? Oh, she asked questions all the time. Veyde would laugh and make up some droll answer. Tiger would try to explain, and would get all mixed up and start working on a picture. I would listen to her—but I never could tell her *why*.

"Yes, she was my friend. How shall I describe her? She looked like those other children of the Gods, children of a Black father and a White mother. Her skin was a light brown, not dark like yours and mine. She had the brow of the Whites, but was tall and slender like the Blacks.

"Yet she was different. She *troubled*. Her thoughts had to reach everywhere, keep everything going—the flight of the clouds, the coming and going of the game. She wanted to know the thoughts of the Guardians and to listen to the voices of the spirits of trees and rocks. As a small girl she would get up in the morning to command the sun to rise. Later on, she gave that up.

"She wanted to do so many things. She wanted to fly! Once she found a dead eagle, and took the wings and tied them to her back. Then she stood on the cliff, ready to take off. I was afraid and begged her to wait, but she jumped, and went straight down into the sea! The wings were torn off and floated on the water. I ran down to the shore to help her. She came up spluttering but she was unharmed. 'It was the wrong bird,' she told me. 'Mine is the dragonfly. I'll know better next time.' That autumn I saw her tinker with pieces of ice from the freezing rock pools, and feared that she would make another try. She didn't, though.

"All the things she thought up—and all the times she hurt herself! I can't tell you how many scares she gave me. Once my father Baywillow felled a tree and lopped off the branches. Then he was called away, and left the log lying on the slope. Avens—she was quite small then—had been looking on, and I could see that she was thinking hard. Suddenly she took another, smaller log and laid it across the big one. Then she took a flying start and threw herself on the small log, so that the whole thing started rolling down. She shot across the rolling log like a javelin from an atlatl and was thrown to the ground and hit by the log. She was covered with blood and cried a little, but though she was black and blue for a whole moon, she was quite pleased in the end. 'I knew it would work,' she told me. I asked her what she meant, and if she had planned to take a beating. 'Of course not,' she said, 'that's not what I meant. You saw how quickly I moved, didn't you?' 'I saw you take a nasty fall,' I told her. 'If that's all you saw, you must be blind,' she said. To this day I don't know what she wanted me to see—unless it was that a girl could shoot herself through the air like a javelin.

"She had a holy place, which she showed me once, late in the summer. It was way up on the sandy beach, where the grass grew short, and there were a lot of mushrooms—more than you could count. They were all standing in a ring, as if they had joined hands for a dance. She made a sign to me to keep out, stepped into the ring, and lay down. Her head touched one side of the ring and her feet the other. I just stood there, wondering. She jumped up and said, 'That ring comes back every summer, and it grows with me. Each summer I am bigger, and the ring is bigger too. As long as it is here, you must not step into it, Whitespear: it's mine and the spirits will go for you. When it is gone, you may walk through it—but don't linger!'

"I was careful to keep outside it. Later on, when the mushrooms were gone, I went to the place and stood there for a while, just to see what would happen. I soon felt scared and had to look around. Then I ran away, but I tripped over a root and hurt my knee. So I knew better than to go back.

"There was one thing Avens couldn't do, and it vexed her. She had no pictures! I was the one who received that gift. When I see an animal, it stays in my soul's eye, and I can call it back, even though many winters have passed. That was the art of Tiger, Avens's father; yet none of those five had it; it passed to me. Oh, she tried hard! When I had made a picture, she tried to do the same, but hers remained wood and stone, where mine came alive. She would ask me to blow a spirit into her picture, but it didn't help. She wanted to know how I did it. I could only tell her that the soul's eye is like a rock pool when the sun is low in the sky: it catches the picture and holds it. 'So it is,' said Avens, 'but for me it stays only for a breath or two. Then comes a shower and blots it out.'

"Still, I think she retained many images that passed others by. 'I am the real mammoth,' she said once. 'The mammoth never forgets, and neither do I.' And so it was."

BISON

The s u n was still hot in the cloudless sky. The sea shimmered tranquilly in the distance, but around the islands the surface was darkened by ripples: the afternoon sea-breeze was coming to life. Veyde was comforting Marigold, who was now happily taking large bites of the raw pike, when suddenly a call was heard. Everyone sprang to attention, for the call meant that large game was in sight. A Black man and a young girl ran into the glade. It was Tiger, Veyde's husband, and their young daughter Mullein.

At this time, Tiger was in his fortieth summer or thereabouts. He was slightly grizzled—early greying ran in his family—but otherwise showed few signs of age. As he slowed from running to a walk, a slight limp became noticeable. That was the memento of a broken leg he had suffered as a youngster, when Veyde had nursed him back to health.

"Bison on the mainland, Miss Veyde," he said, using the formal manner of the Whites. "Miss Mullein saw them."

A whirl of activity set up at once. The Whites took fish and small game on their island, as well as an occasional elk or horse, but what they lived for was the big game on the mainland. For such hunts, their island was in an ideal strategic position. The great herbivores would move along the sweep of shore meadows, which offered excellent grazing, and this could easily be surveyed from Veyde's Island. Then, according to the position of the game, the prevailing wind, and so on, suitable tactics could be worked out. The islanders had the advantage of access by sea, and could raft themselves to a secluded spot to land.

Veyde turned to Mullein with a question, and the girl answered, hesitating over her words as she often did, "They were . . . on Sweetfern Meadow, Mother. They are—they are—b-bachelors . . . I think."

On the landward beach of Veyde's Island was a high promontory from which the mainland coast could be surveyed; it was called Lookout Point. Straight across from it, the mainland tapered into a similar point, but on both sides the flat shore meadows fell off to the southwest and the north. Veyde and Tiger ran up to the summit of Lookout Point, and Mullein and Whitespear followed. Marten was not there. He often went on solitary raids, and usually returned laden with game.

"Good scouting, Miss Mullein," said Tiger. "That is bison, all right. I can see five—no, six, I think."

Dwarfed by the distance, the animals could be seen as dark dots on a background of vivid green. "They do look like a bachelor flock," Veyde commented. "They are all the same size. I think Mister Marten would say so," she finished with motherly pride. Marten's eyesight was a wonder even to his own parents.

In the spring, the bison herds usually broke up into smaller groups. Most consisted of a big bull with his cows and calves, and the variation in size would be evident even at this distance. The young males, on the other hand, tended to form small bachelor flocks. Later in the summer, as the rutting time approached, the scattered groups would rejoin into larger herds, and hunting tactics would change accordingly. In this case, the fact that all the animals were similar in size pointed to a party of young bulls.

"The wind is rising," said Veyde. "That will help." The others nodded. As usual on a sunny afternoon, there would be a sea-wind. A party moving inside the forest, sheltered from view by the thick fringe of alders, would not be betrayed by its scent. "We are really going to need your help this time, more than ever," Veyde told Tiger and looked at the others with a smile. Again they nodded, fully aware of their responsibilities.

The Whites' normal tactics in bison hunting were based upon their own favorite weapons. They were rather clumsy at throwing spears, and the atlatl, or throwing-stick, was quite foreign to them. They preferred to come to grips at close quarters, working in pairs, one using a tremendous broad-bladed sticking-spear, the other a heavy hand-axe. To do this, they often had to provoke their quarry to attack them, for even the Whites, who were capable of almost incredible bursts of speed over a short range, were rarely able to hunt down a bison once it had turned tail. A big bull defending his harem or a cow defending her calf could usually be induced to approach. Young bachelor bulls, on the other hand, were notoriously nervous and unpredictable. Even so, by putting one pair of hunters on each flank Veyde felt that she could probably intercept one or two fleeing bulls. Even without the help of Tiger and his atlatl throwers, Veyde's party would have been pretty sure of bagging two or three animals. With his help and some luck, they would bag them all.

Tiger, Whitespear, Avens, and Mullein were all expert atlatl hunters. Marten, of course, was an expert in every kind of hunting, but no one knew when he might return. At the expected range, the light javelins were not likely to kill an animal outright, except for a very lucky throw. If you could get close enough, and a bison were courteous enough to present himself broadside, you could pierce his heart . . . but, as Marten summed it up, bison weren't very courteous. What the javelins could do was maim an animal, or perhaps enrage it enough to draw an attack, which was precisely what Veyde wanted. Any seriously wounded animal could then be left till later, while the Whites concentrated on the uninjured ones.

As everybody knew, even the best-laid plan could come to nought. A curious crow or a frightened woodcock might betray the presence of the hunters and scare the bison into a stampede. Such things were in the hands of the Guardians, and to the Guardians the Whites directed their prayers. For their own safety no prayers were offered. They went about their work with proud fatalism.

The routine had been perfected during years of coopera-tion. It was only necessary for Veyde to give a few orders, which she framed as polite requests. A party of eight Whites boarded the raft and started to paddle across the channel. There were also two small coracles. The art of constructing these had reached Veyde's Island in bygone times, by strange routes, from the people of the Salt Sea on the other side of their world. Mullein took one and Avens the other, while Tiger and Whitespear jumped into the water and swam across. The group collected on the mainland promontory, the arms were distributed, and the party took off.

·   ·   ·

They plunged through the forest in single file. The path was old and well worn for they had used it innumerable times on similar expeditions, and it skirted the beach at a safe dis-tance. Covered with light-brown pine needles, it undulated through the vegetation in long curves: neither men nor animals move in a straight line through the forest.

Trudging along, Whitespear thought he could sense the rising elation of his White friends, even though they moved in absolute silence. His own heart was beating faster; he was suffused by pleasurable excitement. Yet at the same time he was conscious of something much deeper growing within those silent striding figures, of mounting tensions that were beyond him, powers he could never match. It was as if in every man or woman a little flame of passion had been fanned to life and now slowly blossomed higher and higher. It shone as a small terrible light in those ice-blue eyes, which seemed already to be seeking out some overwhelming consummation ahead. Stronger and stronger burned the flame, carefully nourished and carefully restrained. Already they were walking in a world of their own, one that he could never enter: they were rushing to their fulfillment, to their fate, to their doom. They radiated the splendor of a coming achievement of unthinkable grimness and joy. He shivered. He knew what he was going to witness, and he knew that his gentle White friends were now a race apart.

They stopped to separate. As Veyde moved away, she turned to look back at Tiger. She was grave and erect in the majesty of her passion. Love and valediction fought in her eyes.

Now the atlatl party was alone, and it crept stealthily shoreward. The sea flashed myriads of sparks through the alder leaves, and they stopped. The bulls were there, within range, like great boulders scattered on the meadow with its lush grass and patches of intensely colored flowers—purple heartsease, blue tufted vetch, yellow birdsfoot trefoil and buttercup, and massed chickweed like living snowdrifts under the sea-wind.

Tiger, with small hand movements, assigned his party their targets.

The animals were at their ease, lethargic in the heat.

Horseflies buzzed incessantly, and the great beasts reacted with lazy jerks of the skin. The rich scent of cattle tickled Whitespear's nostrils. The bulls had finished shedding and were smart and sleek in their summer pelage, its reddish-grey tones set off by the jet-black manes and dark heads. They did not yet have the massiveness of the older bulls, but Whitespear sensed their tremendous weight and power and the menace of their proud horns, wickedly curved at the point. His inner eye was absorbing the sight; he knew that pictures were forming within him. Then he felt a hand on his arm and looked back to meet Tiger's eyes. He knew then that his experience was being shared. Tiger raised his atlatl, and they all jumped through the alders, found their balance, and threw.

They scored four hits. Tiger's javelin smashed through the left shoulder blade of a bull, through the vertebral spines and into the right shoulder blade, where it remained fixed, jamming both forelegs in the position of a beginning canter. A second bull, turning to flee, was hit by Mullein in the abdomen, but this did not stop it. It thundered away, closely followed by another with Whitespear's missile sticking out of its face. Avens's javelin passed clean through the lower part of her quarry's neck, causing little damage, and the animal reared up on its hind legs.

They had time for a second throw before the bulls were out of range, and this time Avens scored a decisive hit. The bull crashed down, rolled over, and started to get up again. But now the bolts were shot, and already the Whites, four pairs of them, had burst out of the forest and closed in at superhuman speed. Once again Whitespear was witnessing the final and incredible transformation of the gentle Whitefolk. In a supreme fighting madness they rushed their quarry, and things happened so fast that only disjointed pictures of unrelated events flashed into his eyes and fixed themselves in his brain. At one moment, three bulls collided bodily with the humans who flung themselves on them, dexterously ducking the sweep of the horns. The animals were stuck, battered, clawed by strong hands clutching at their manes, their horns, their tails; they crumpled, toppled over, and were destroyed. Another picture remained in him, without his grasping its meaning; that of a fourth bull, the one nicked by Avens's first missile, fleeing thunderously, its great horn, scythelike, splitting the head of a stumbling human. There was still the bull paralyzed by Tiger's bolt, and now the torrent of raging humanity fell on it and brought it down. Two bulls, one of them wounded, had got away; later on they would track the wounded one.

Such was the fury and strength of these great hunters, such their disregard of any danger, that Whitespear always felt utterly overawed. Never, he thought, could he perform such feats.

The Whites rose, their breasts heaving in great gasping breaths, their faces contorted masks of painful labor, mouth gaping, eyes unseeing.

Then their eyes came into focus and their gaze swept the scene. Slowly they raised their arms, still shaking from the effort. And now came the laughter, thunderous, uproarious laughter. They had conquered. They had done the impossible. It was their supreme moment. They had unleashed all that savage ferocity which, it was ordained, should always lie in readiness somewhere deep in their being, for all their gentle everyday ways. They were triumphant beasts of prey. They looked into each other's flaming eyes, and they laughed, and laughed, and laughed.

 HELLEBORINE

"That was how I came to visit Blue Lake," White-spear told Oriole, "and how Avens found a new thing to worry about. For on that bison hunt, my father Baywillow was badly hurt. His scalp was split open, and beneath the wound his skull was soft to the touch. He was carried unconscious to the raft and ferried back to the island.

"Miss Bracken was our healer. She had been taught by old Silverbirch the sage, who died when I was still a small boy. But she said there was little she could do for my father—she did not know enough. She had only had two years' apprenticeship with Mister Silverbirch, after his rightful successor was lost on the ice.

"Silverbirch had told her once that he had taught his eldest son all that he knew. That man, whose name was Helleborine, was reputed to live at Blue Lake, a settlement of inland

Whites. Perhaps, Miss Bracken said, he could be induced to come to Veyde's Island to help us.

"Baywillow, meanwhile, had recovered so far that he could take some food and drink. But he was in a daze, didn't seem to hear our words, and could say nothing. A council was called between Miss Hind my mother, Miss Veyde and Mister Tiger, Miss Bracken, and myself. As always, Tiger and I had to interpret between Hind and Veyde, for neither spoke the other's language and they were as different as night and day. Yet this time they were in accord. They agreed that I should go and seek the help of Mister Helleborine, the healer of Blue Lake. I, of course, was eager to go, and everybody was cheered by the thought of Mister Helleborine and his healing powers, for my father was greatly loved among the people of the island.

"I told Avens about my mission, and she promptly declared that she was going too—as I had hoped. Although Blue Lake was only one day's journey from our cloudberry bogs, where I had been many times, I had never been to the village. In the old days there had been much intercourse between the islanders and the Bluelakers, but that was winters ago, in Silverbirch's time. So we knew only what we had been told by our elders: that it was a large village and was governed by a divine Black man who had fathered many Browns—children of the Gods, as the Whites called them. Tiger had known him as a very large, fat man with much wind in his belly and many words in his mouth. Goshawk was his name. All this sounded very exciting and, to an inexperienced boy, just a little frightening, so I was glad to have Avens with me.

"We reached the lake on the third day of our journey, and spotted the village on the other side. There were a lot of tents and many people moving about. We were still too far away to see what they looked like. I wondered what they would say when two strangers—a Black man and a Brown girl—turned up among all these Whites, and whether they would be friendly. Still, Tiger had assured me that the Whites of Blue Lake were just as kind and gentle as those of Veyde's Island, so I forgot my qualms. We skirted the lake and approached the village.

"And then it was all different!

"Suddenly there was a woman in front of us. She held a big spear in her right hand, and raised her left to bar our way. She was a Brown woman, like Avens, but older. She started to speak to us in White, but seeing me she switched to the Black language. She didn't speak it well, but I could understand her. She was asking us what we were doing there, and she did not sound friendly at all.

"When I told her about our mission, she appeared mollified. She said that they had to be vigilant because there were evil powers afoot in the forest. This they had been told by their Divine Father Goshawk, who knew all things and had once won a great victory over Shelk, the Master of Evil. The story I had heard was rather different, but I didn't care to tell her that, for I was anxious to meet Mister Helleborine. She said yes, Mister Helleborine lived here, and we could see him, if the Divine Father permitted us to do so. But first of all we had to be brought to the Great One, with whom the decision rested.

"While this Brown woman took us through the village, I realized that there was something else quite different from what I had expected: the people. I had heard that this was a White village, but in fact there were only a few Whites; most of the people were Brown.

"Yet the most uncanny thing about the place was that there were *no children*. No children! Can you imagine? A whole village with no children at all. No running, no playing, no laughter, no curious eyes, no welcoming grins, no eager voices asking who we were, where we came from, and where we were going. We saw a couple of youngsters, maybe ten winters old. They were together, and yet without togetherness, if you see what I mean. They did not speak to each other. They looked at us dully, without interest.

"It was a busy place, and people were moving about, but I heard nobody speak. They seemed to be walking in a dream. They were like ghosts searching hopelessly for something they had lost while still alive. I felt myself shudder. The village was under a blight, you could sense it; and yet none of them seemed to realize it.

"I had been told that the people of Blue Lake were just as well-mannered and kindly as those of Veyde's Island. Yet the behavior of this Brown woman would have drawn strong censure among us. She hardly even nodded at the other people whom we met, and the Whites might have been thin air as far as she was concerned.

"There was an old White woman who was standing by a tent and nibbling on a fish. She was facing the other way and didn't see us. But the Brown woman thought she was in her way and pushed her aside, so that she stumbled and fell. Nobody took any notice, and the Brown woman simply walked on, not bothering to look back. I saw Avens's face turn ashen and knew that she was as shocked as I.

"Still, we were now going to see the Divine Father, the great ruler of Blue Lake. The woman had taken us through the entire village, but she kept on walking. She told us that Goshawk lived apart from mortal men."

.   .   .

The lord of Blue Lake was perched on a high stool in the shade of a tree. The place had been carefully chosen to give him a view of the tents and the lake, yet ensure his privacy. There he could rest, his great presence felt but not seen, his divine power inspiring the heart of every one of his children. So the Brown woman told Whitespear and Avens, impressing them with the honor about to be conferred upon them:

to be allowed to meet Goshawk face to face. Deeply awed, Whitespear looked forward to seeing a great old sage.

The chair was indeed a magnificent throne, with a back and elbow-rests, covered by a bearskin; but the divine Goshawk turned out to be a bent, paunchy, toothless old man, scantily clad in a loincloth which did not improve his appearance. His eyes stared into space, and his face had the utter inscrutability of obese old age. Nothing could be read from his features, blurred as they were by pouch and jowl, flabby and hanging. Once magnificently fat, Goshawk was wasting away in his old age. Whitespear was unpleasantly reminded of the part-mummified cadaver of a seal that he had found once on the shore of Veyde's Island.

But on his lap rested the carved wooden staff, mark of his lordship, and the Brown woman bowed low. She spoke in her oddly accented version of the Black tongue.

"Divine Father," she said, "I bring two visitors who ask to pay homage to you."

Goshawk's vacant stare came slowly into focus, and he gripped his staff. Whitespear noted that there was a small flap of skin tied to its end, and suspected that it was mainly used to whisk away flies, of which there were plenty. Goshawk's small mouth moved.

"Thank you, my girl," he said. His voice was flat and almost inaudible. "Good girl. What did you say, now?"

She repeated her words, and the bleary gaze was turned on the strangers.

"Oh yes, oh yes," said Goshawk hurriedly. "You are welcome, I'm sure. Why," he went on, taking Whitespear in, "you are Black. How nice. You speak a civilized tongue. I'll see that you get a skin of wine and a bitch for the night. Yes . . . A skin . . ." His voice trailed away and he blinked several times, as if trying to rouse himself from sleep.

"I bring you greetings from Tiger, my father's brother," said Whitespear politely. Goshawk stirred a little.

"Tiger? Oh yes, Tiger. Of course. My oldest guest-friend. How pleasant. My dear young fellow, you are welcome. See that you get something to eat, you look emaciated. Tell them to give you some of my venison. Yes, I insist." In the midst of his babbling, Goshawk fell asleep. Avens nudged White-spear, who said loudly:

"Sir, I ask your permission to see Mister Helleborine, the healer of Blue Lake."

Goshawk came to with a start. "Very good," he said, nodding several times. "You are welcome. Civilized tongue. Good to hear. So you are a healer, eh?"

The Brown woman touched Whitespear's arm. "We must not tire him," she said firmly. "I will take you to Mister Helleborine."

It was at this point that Avens lost her temper, an occur-rence so unusual that Whitespear was left gaping. Waving her fists, she screamed at the lord of Blue Lake, "You terrible old man, this is all your doing!" The Brown woman, thun-derstuck, gripped her spear. But the grotesque old man on his perch seemed gratified. He looked with new interest at the incensed girl.

"Spirited girl you have got there, young man," he said appreciatively. "Who is she?"

"She is Avens daughter of Veyde and Tiger, sir," said Whitespear. The old man, now thoroughly awake and ap-parently enjoying himself, nodded and turned to Avens.

"Yes, my dear, you are right. I am a very terrible man." Suddenly a gleeful imp looked out of his eyes, and he leered toothlessly at Avens. "Have I not vanquished the fearsome Shelk? Have I not fathered a new breed of man?"

"What you have fathered is living death," said Avens, trembling with rage.

"You are the same breed," Goshawk pointed out with a supercilious air.

"A sickness on my breed," said Avens rudely, and Whitespear found himself wondering where she got her sayings from. "No life quickens within it. We are all living dead."

"It will come yet. It is up to you." Goshawk broke into wheezing laughter. The Brown woman, still completely bewildered, was looking from him to Avens and back, but at a gesture from Goshawk she drew away a few paces. Clearly, Goshawk was hugely amused, and Whitespear realized that the old man had been utterly bored and was delighted to meet someone who was not obsequious. Avens had now regained her composure and spoke coldly:

"I wish death on you. It is Black men like you who breed the living dead, who breed men and women like myself, doomed to be childless. Here in your village I have seen the horror you are bringing into the world. Yes, I wish death on you, and on all your kind."

"And on your father?"

She was silent, and Goshawk laughed again. "I can see that you are thinking, but I'm thinking too. I am a thinker!" He put his finger to his forehead and made a sly face. Then he beamed at Avens with open friendliness. "Yes," he said meditatively, "I have lived, and I have made my mark. Now it is up to you. And I mean *you*."

Their gazes interlocked. Not for long; at his last words, her pose slackened, and she shrugged. "Yes, you have made your mark," she said slowly. "Ten winters ago for the last time, I reckon." She smiled unpleasantly.

"Impudent girl," Goshawk murmured uncertainly. He raised his staff and shooed away an obtrusive fly. Then he seemed to come to a decision. "Go and see Mister Helleborine. Then come back to me. I have something to tell you."

Avens, who had apparently lost interest, had already turned her back, and Whitespear hurriedly took his leave. Goshawk was clucking with laughter again as they left.

.   .   .

The Brown woman took them to the outskirts of the village and pointed to a path into the forest. She now looked at Avens with open suspicion, as if expecting her to become violent at any moment, and clearly wanted to get rid of them as soon as possible. In brief words she told them that they would find Mister Helleborine in the woods. Whitespear, somewhat intimidated by her curt manner, ventured to ask what he was doing there.

"Communicating with the spirits," answered the woman without any show of interest. Her disdain was patent: the eccentricities of the Whites were beneath her notice.

"How shall we find him in the forest?"

"You will hear him," she told them and turned away.

Avens started off without looking back, and Whitespear followed her. She seemed sunk in thought, and he had glimpsed a forbidding expression in her face. In contrast with her usual manner, she did not turn her head even once to speak to him over her shoulder, and they trudged on in silence. The road took them through pinewoods filled with birdsong and across mossy knolls, until suddenly they heard a high-pitched scream, as from somebody in extreme agony. It was repeated, and repeated again. Then silence; even the birds were silent. Then, once more, the eerie screams were heard.

"That must be Mister Helleborine," said Whitespear, awed. "He must be calling to the dead."

Avens did not answer for a while. Finally she said, "Yes. But to which dead?"

They found the old healer sitting in a small glade, leaning back on a mossy rock. His face was raised to the sun and his eyes were closed. As they approached, he opened his mouth and uttered once more that tremendous cry, a call to distant worlds, which seemed to reverberate from the very sky. It shook Whitespear to the core of his being, and he covered his ears. That voice must surely penetrate to the soul-birds' abode itself, to that faraway land where the spirits of the Whites soared after death.

Then the healer became aware of them. He rose courteously, as if nothing special had happened, and made the Whites' gesture of greeting, passing his hands over his eyes.

To Whitespear and Avens, Mister Helleborine son of Speedwell and Silverbirch was an old man. His face was gaunt and lined, but firm and full of repose, like that of somebody at peace with the world. His eyes were startlingly blue and piercing. In many ways he reminded Whitespear of old Silverbirch, the sage of his boyhood, but the color of his eyes must have come from his mother: Silverbirch had been grey-eyed.

They found him a kindly and courteous man, very different from the peremptory Brown woman. He listened with interest to Whitespear's tale and immediately declared himself ready to go with them to the island—if the divine Goshawk would permit him to do so. Helleborine's quiet composure and friendliness were highly reassuring to Whitespear, who felt that he was back to normal after a day in a topsy-turvy world.

So they returned to the village, to find Goshawk still perched on his high stool and seemingly fast asleep. There was a complete hush about the place. Nobody was in sight: the Black God of Blue Lake had been left to slumber in peace. "Do we have to wake him?" asked Whitespear, who would have preferred to leave right away. But Helleborine went up to the throne and looked into the bloated face. For a moment he stood motionless, then he passed his hands over his face, mumbled an inaudible word, and stretched out a finger to prod the Black God.

The stool and the sitting figure toppled over grotesquely, and Goshawk fell in a heap to the ground.

"By the Mammoth," whispered Whitespear to Avens, "he

is dead." It seemed all the more horrifying because the im-
pact on the thick moss-cover was so silent. Yet his first
thought was: Now we'll never know what he wanted to tell
Avens.

The healer bent over the twisted corpse. His large hands
moved gently over its breast. He rose in silence. Then, to
Whitespear's shock and amazement, he did something the
young man had never seen before. Very deliberately, he spat
into the dead face.

Avens suddenly broke into a paroxysm of sobs. She stumbled forward, blinded by tears, and threw herself into Helleborine's arms, embracing him in a passion of pity and
sympathy.

Helleborine disengaged himself gently. "We must go
away, Miss Avens," he said.

"The blight is lifted! The blight is lifted!" Avens cried.
"Mister Helleborine, can you not wake them all to life? It is
over! The sun is back in the sky! The curse is gone, Mister
Helleborine!"

"And why do you think I have been calling in the forest?"
said the healer. "It is only the beginning. We must go, Miss
Avens, before they come and find him."

"They must be awakened!"

"You understand much, Miss Avens, but not everything.
This is not the time. They would not understand. We must
go. The time will come."

She looked into his kindly blue eyes and seemed to take
hold of herself. "Yes, we must go," she said.

They went without looking back, and the first flies settled
on the Black God of Blue Lake.

.   .   .

"I can see now," Whitespear told Oriole, "that the estrange-
ment between Avens and me began with that journey back
to Veyde's Island. And it was no doing of mine. She kept by

Helleborine's side, and between them they spoke much, but they lowered their voices when I drew near, so I knew they didn't want me to hear. I felt also that the courteous old man suffered because of this. From time to time he would turn to me with an apology—oh, he reminded me very much of fussy old Silverbirch, his father. Once, when Avens had stopped to pick strawberries, he even told me that he and Avens were struggling in spirit. He said that the road of her life, from one breath to the next, had risen up in front of her like the face of a cliff, and she despaired of walking it. She would need his help, he said, and his heart was heavy for her. Yet I did not know which way her thoughts and feelings had been turning. I was still a boy with little knowledge of the world, and the turmoil of real suffering was still locked in my future, unknown to me. No, I should have understood, from Avens's words to Goshawk and from Helleborine's words to me, that some momentous resolution had been forced upon her, and that she now contemplated acts and deeds so great and gruesome as to make her heart quake. At that point Avens rejoined us and Helleborine fell silent. Later on I asked Avens what was the matter, but she turned away, and the healer only looked glum and perplexed.

"All this was driven out of my head when we came to the island. The healer examined Baywillow my father, and you could see that he was a great man and knew his trade. Bracken, who was elated by the presence of such a master healer, hung on his every movement and word, and they conferred at length. We didn't understand much of what they said. All through the examination my father uttered not a single word, but there was a look of understanding in his eyes.

"In the end Helleborine gave us his verdict. He said that the injury was beyond his powers. He thought he could nurse my father back to bodily health, but to give him back his living spirit, a greater knowledge was needed. He reminded us of Shelk, the master devil who had also been a master healer: 'Shelk had two guises: an evil one in which he destroyed everyone and everything, and a good one in which he was the greatest healer on earth. I do not believe that his powers vanished forever when he died. The powers of evil are still here for sure, and so, I believe, are the powers of good. Maybe they must be united in another such supreme dealer of woe and consolation; I do not know. Is there anybody here with the youth, strength, and boldness of heart to go out on a quest?'

"His eyes turned to me. 'I know that Shelk received his powers from a grand old magician who lived in the ancient days on the coast of the Salt Sea. It is known, too, that Shelk had a foster-brother: a man called Fox. It is barely possible that the gift was passed on to him or to his issue. Alas, I do not know where Fox went.'

"At the mention of Fox, Tiger's eyes lit up. He rose to his feet and lifted his arms: 'Fox was my enemy, but he became my friend. I know where he went. For some time he made his home with a Black tribe at Big Lake, which lies far to the west. Then he moved to the Salt Sea. He has sons and daughters. If you think they can help us, Mister Helleborine, it is our duty to find them.'

"Cautiously Helleborine replied, 'I may be wrong, but I have no other advice for you.'

"Any one of us would gladly have trekked to the end of the world for Baywillow's sake. 'He is my brother,' said Tiger, 'but he is Whitespear's father, and Whitespear has the youth. He also has something else that will stand him in good stead.' I did not know then what Tiger meant, but it is clear to me now: my pictures would help me, as Tiger well knew.

"I was eager to go. What excitement! I would see the world. I would travel far and wide, perhaps even to the Salt Sea at the other side of the world, far, far to the west, where I was told the sun set into a brinier water than ours.

"But where to start? Tiger knew: 'The place to start is the

big meeting that the Black peoples hold every summer under the full moon when the nights come back. It is held in the glade of the Sacred Pines, and I will teach you the way. I know all the landmarks.'

"After that there were many talks with Tiger and with Hind my mother in preparation for the journey. Helleborine the healer stayed with us to work with Baywillow, and Bracken followed him everywhere. He taught her much about healing plants that she did not know or had forgotten. I remember valerian for palpitations and bearberry for making water.

"Then, more than a moon after the summer solstice, came the day when the moon-stick told us I had to set out. I would have asked Avens to come along, but she had slipped away. It was to be a longer journey than I had imagined; and as I was to find out later, during all of it Avens would be there, unseen by me, unknown to me, moving mysteriously in the dark, bent on her own ends, which were revealed to me summers afterwards. Oh yes, she knew very well what she was doing. But for myself, I started out on my own to make the Summer Meet for the first time in my life.

"That was the beginning of a new life for me. I was young and strong. I had no fears. I went along eagerly, expecting much, knowing little and caring less. What I did not know was that when I started out to find the tracks of Shelk the Healer, Avens had already gone forth to find those of Shelk the Destroyer."

 OTTER

The S u m m e r Meet had been held in the same place for generations ever since the neighboring tribes of Big Lake and Swidden Moor had met there to settle a dispute over hunting rights. Soon other tribes were taking part. It became an important center for dealers in flintwork, castoreum, skins, and ivory, for artists wishing to exchange their work for other goods, for itinerant shamans and apprentices looking for a position with a chief, and for anybody who wanted to meet people and listen to news and stories. In particular esteem were the traders in flintwork from the far South, for their merchandise was almost priceless in this land of granite and gneiss. They were well received and business was brisk. Old friends met and embraced. Bashful, newly initiated young men were introduced to chiefs and hunters of great repute. Marriages were contracted and disputes were settled, amicably or by man-to-man combat. The proceedings were enlivened by sports and dances and a hornful or two of the famous black wine, brewed with loving care by experts.

The Meet was held under the first full moon of late summer, when the nights were lengthening and her full brilliance was again revealed. The place was a big, flat, treeless knoll overlooking a small lake in which the silver of the moon was caught among the water lilies. In the middle of the glade was a gigantic pyramid-shaped boulder, erected by some prodigious hero of the past. In the stories he was nameless, but he was so big that his full beard covered the glade. The flat sides of the boulder were decorated with paintings, and it was often scaled by adventurous spirits who wanted to put their handprints in ochre on the top.

But the greatest miracle was the stand of larches that sheltered the northern edge of the glade. This tree, which was rare in the area, was called by a name signifying "the-pine-that-dies-in-the-autumn-and-comes-to-life-in-the-spring." It was a holy tree, and nobody knew of a grove that equaled this one. The trees came to life in the spring with the miraculous appearance of tender green needles. With undiminished beauty, they turned a soft brown in the autumn. Then the needles were shed, and the place became an abode of death, watched over by grim skeleton trees and entered by nobody.

Now, in late summer, Whitespear found it a lively place. Here for the first time he found himself in an all-Black society. He listened to the buzzing of strident voices in his own mother tongue with a sense partly of exhilaration, partly of diffidence, as he passed groups of men standing in discussion or reclining at ease, refreshing themselves from large bison horns. He had rarely heard the Black language spoken with this kind of self-assurance and sheer exuberance. On Veyde's Island, it was a private language for those who mastered it, and it was immediately abandoned in conversation at the presence of Whites, in deference to their inability to speak it.

The Meet was an all-male affair, conducted by the men while their women and children were busy with the berry harvest. The only exceptions were a few female shamans and healers, usually of mature years and rarely attractive enough to cause men to perform silly feats in order to impress them. In all that gathering Whitespear saw only one woman, whom he recognized as a shaman from the red Sun-symbol on her brow.

The sun was already low in the sky. Whitespear's attention was caught by a man standing upright in front of a reclining group and speaking insistently. He seemed to be talking as much with his hands as with his mouth. They fluttered about, sometimes jerkily, sometimes with soft, caressing movements; then they met and were wrung together as if squeezing the last drop out of a skin of wine; then again they flapped out in all directions.

All of the resting men held horns in their hands. A big man on a pile of skins, who appeared to be a chief, raised his horn to his lips, and at the sight of it Whitespear drew closer. He saw that it was a masterpiece of the carver's art. The annuli had been filed away, leaving a smooth surface on which figures had been carved. He could see one: an otter with a fish in its mouth and its tail running into the long apex of the horn. His heart rose, for he thought he recognized the pattern. On an impulse, he stepped up and spoke to the big man:

"Excuse me, sir, but may I introduce myself? I am Whitespear of Veyde's Island, and I am admiring the drinking-vessel in your hand."

The man looked quizzically at him. "No mean name, by the Mammoth. I, as anybody here could tell you, am Otter of Swidden Moor. Are you coveting my horn?"

"Indeed I am not, Otter," said Whitespear, taken aback. "I can see your totem on this side of it. Is it possible that there is a fox on the other?"

"Ho!" said Otter. "A man who can see around corners."

He turned the horn around, and Whitespear smiled. "That earns you a draught, young man. Sit down and drink with me." He handed Whitespear the vessel. "The horn is mine, though, and will remain so. Dear old Jay here, who flutters his wings so cleverly, has been bartering for it since we came. I tell you, Jay, all the flints in your land will not win you my horn."

The dealer wrung his hands as if in a passion, but did not answer. Whitespear returned the horn. "Flints?" he said. "I could do with some." He felt about in his pack and pulled out another horn, which he held up for Jay to see. There was a gasp from the entire party. Jay's hands seemed to freeze to each other. Otter took the horn, turned it over and over, and sighed. It was smaller than his own, but of exquisite workmanship. On its polished surface a fish and a seal seemed to swim towards its rim, the seal belly upward in relation to the fish (as any sealer would tell you), while an eel, facing the other way, wound itself around the apex.

"I could have sworn by the mammoth's Guardian that there was only one man who could do a thing like this," said Otter. "It is almost as good as mine—almost, but not quite! Mine was given to my father Fox when I was still a young boy: given in friendship from a former enemy who became a friend, and who was the greatest artist in the land."

"And whose name was Tiger," said Whitespear. "I know the story."

"He made this one too?"

"No. I did. You're right: it isn't quite as good as Tiger's work. But he taught me; and he said that this would fetch a round of first-rate flints."

Otter's face was alight with interest. "We heard that Tiger went back to an island with his Whites. Is that where you hail from? Are you by any chance a son of Tiger's?"

"He is my father's brother."

Otter's gaze went from Whitespear to Jay. "Well, Jay,

what do you say? How many javelin points will you give him for this?"

Jay's restless hands shot out and took the vessel. He turned it over and over, scrutinizing it keenly in the luminous twilight. "Would you care to come with me, Whitespear?" he asked. His respectful manner was eloquent.

Otter nudged Whitespear. "You can trust him, my boy. I know him: he comes every year. Crooked dealers are only seen once!" He laughed at this adage. "Come back when your business is finished. You have much to tell me."

. . .

From far away in the slowly gathering twilight came the bark of a bull shelk, repeated twice. It was a deep, hoarse sound, but with a yapping overtone which gave it great carrying power. Whitespear and Jay exchanged glances, and Jay smiled. "No hunting tonight," he said. "They have been looking too deep into the horns."

He started to open his unwieldy packs. "Hard work, lugging all these rocks from the Land of Flints," he observed, while his dexterous hands flashed about as if detached from his body. "I don't travel alone. No, no, my boy! There are ruffians about. We go from village to village, I and my helpers. They are good and strong, and wield a javelin as well as the next man.

"Now, my boy. I'm not a thief, and Chief Otter will vouch for me, as will anybody else at the Meet. I have gone the rounds for many a summer and they know they can trust me. A crooked dealer comes to a bad end." Jay swiveled around, squatted on his haunches, and looked Whitespear in the eye. "Let me tell you this: what you have here is worth my best stuff, which I carry myself. I have two helpers, and their flints are good too, but mine are the best. Take your time. The choice is yours."

He was laying out an array of points, knives, engraving tools, and harpoons. For the second time that evening Whitespear was taken aback. He had seen very few pieces of the work of the master flint-knappers of the South. The idea that his own handiwork could be measured against such things seemed incredible. He kept a straight face nevertheless and made a bold selection, beginning with the most beautiful javelin-point of them all. He pored over the exhibits, encouraged by approving grunts from the dealer.

"That is about right, I judge," said Jay finally.

"It's all I need and can carry," said Whitespear.

"If that is so, I will stem my curiosity. Doubtless you have other treasures like this horn. No, do not show them. I cannot pay for them. I wanted a noble drinking-vessel for my chief, and now I have it. Now I want glutton skins—you don't have any, do you? No, I see you don't. Well, my boy, remember that there are men who will kill for a thing like this." He tapped the horn with his fingers.

"Then I was lucky to meet you."

"You were. And you were well advised to show this one only, and in a closed company. No violence is allowed at the Meet, but you cannot curb the tongues of spies and informers. Anyway, you will be safe with Otter—from *that* kind of danger."

Whitespear cast a sharp glance at the dealer. "Do you foresee other kinds, Jay?"

The man from the South grinned boyishly. "No danger for your life, at any rate," he said. "But come! We must broach this horn with a drop of black wine."

They sat down to drink, Whitespear squatting in the manner of the Whites while Jay reclined, resting his back against his bag of goods. "Yes, I am an old hand," he said. "I made my first journey to the Meet as a beardless boy. I went with my father then, who was a trader like me, and back home at Birchneck Village, in the Land of Flints, my sons are waiting their turn. In our land the flint grows in the rock, and good flintwork is cheap; but the yellow firestone is precious, and I buy that in the North. I also buy glutton skins, which are much coveted in our land, so that our wolverines are all but extinct. There is nothing better than glutton skin in the everlasting wet snow of our winters.

"I start my journey just before the summer solstice. It takes two moons, Whitespear, and then I have my landmarks and roads, and know every slingshot-length of the trip, so as not to lose any time. Everywhere I'm made welcome and treated as the equal of chiefs and shamans. Up South, in the sun direction, the villages are close together, less than a day apart. Here, they lie more sparsely, and my welcome is even warmer; many a solitary woman makes me a bed. To be a journeying tradesman is a good life, Whitespear: you ought to try it."

Whitespear smiled. The suggestion seemed utterly absurd to him. "I have been set a task, Jay," he said, "and I must go with Otter."

"A pity," Jay commented. "We two, you and I, could have traveled together. I have seen what you can do with your hands. Perhaps some other time. I shall look for you at the Meet next summer."

.   .   .

When Whitespear returned to Otter, a ball game had started in the gathering dusk. Men from Swidden Moor were competing with a team from Big Lake, reinforced by two nimble boys from faraway Falcon Hill. The spectators, flushed by hornfuls of black wine, screamed encouragement and ribald comments. Otter, still seated on his pile of skins, welcomed the young man. "The Biglakers are a bit the worse for wear," he observed. "Those Falcon Hill boys are pretty good, though."

The point of the game was to keep possession of the ball, and the Falcon Hill boys were performing feats of dribbling between them. Somebody stumbled, and a thunderous laugh arose. "Look at him—graceful as a rhino dancing in a bog!" "Don't sit on it—you'll burst it!" "Here comes Stoat, swift and vengeful as a lame horse!" Whitespear, reared among the decorous Whites, was amused and slightly shocked.

Otter said, "We know most people at the Meet, but there are bands of ruffians in the forest. No summer without a mosquito," he added sententiously. Noting Whitespear's questioning glance, he launched into an explanation.

The "ruffians," it seemed, were small bands of lawless people hunting in other tribes' territories. Some of them were harmless enough. Not far from the meeting ground, for instance, lived a man with his woman and children, presumably because he liked to live that way (but a loner never bags a mammoth, Otter pointed out). On the other hand, there were the wolfmen, who killed for fun; one band of them had terrorized the Falcon Hill tribe winters ago and had had to be hunted down and destroyed. (When the Guardian sleeps, Man has to take a hand.) But most were just small groups of outcasts trying to make a living. The ordinary hunter would be perfectly safe from them, but a man with a heavy pack might be robbed and maybe killed as well to stop his mouth. (Dead men's voices do not carry far.)

"So you see, Whitespear, I don't like the idea of you walking off alone. Would you care to come with me to Swidden Moor after the Meet?"

"I thank you, Otter, but I have been set a task, and you may be able to help me. I have been looking for the kin of Fox, for my father's sake." And Whitespear told Otter of Baywillow's plight and about the words of Helleborine the healer.

"Your fortune is good," said Otter. "Now, who is the lucky man? Why, he who throws his spear into the thicket and finds that he has killed a deer." Otter seemed to have an unlimited store of old saws at hand. "Well, in a way you have not struck your deer as yet. I am Fox's son, but I never had any interest in shaman work. Our Shaman at Swidden Moor, though, may be able to help you. He was taught by Shelk himself.''

This was great news to Whitespear, who immediately started to ply Otter with questions. However, the Chief seemed strangely reluctant to enlarge upon the theme. Apart from the information that the shaman was called Harrier and, as he said, "kept his own counsel," Whitespear got little out of him. The moon had now climbed high in the sky, and the ballplayers grew tired and lay down to sleep. A slightly tipsy man appeared in front of Otter and handed him a small bird's nest. "Late-breeding wagtail, Chief," he said and stood wavering. "You have the eyes of a lynx, my friend," said Otter and popped one of the fledglings into his mouth. "Will you share my meal, Whitespear?"

Whitespear declined politely. He had grown up among the Whites, to whom most young birds were taboo. Otter nodded understandingly. "The horse eats the grass, but the stag eats the leaves," he said with an air of profundity. "But now let us sleep, for there is much to do in the days to come. I heard a shelk barking this night; if the Guardian wills, we'll smoke his tongue tomorrow. And after the Meet, you will join us for Swidden Moor."

.   .   .

The people of Swidden Moor lived by a beaver-dammed lake, the biggest of its kind known to anybody. It had its name, Horn Lake, because it curved and tapered like a bison's horn. It was quite shallow, apart from the old riverbed along its middle, and the beavers must have worked for untold generations to create the mighty dam. They were often seen mending it, wherever the rush of water suggested a weak point.

The lake, Whitespear was told, was immensely rich in birdlife. According to Otter, the entire tribe could have lived off bird eggs throughout the summer, if so inclined. Now the summer was drawing to an end. The last swifts were gone, a few avocets passed by on the way south, and of the teeming life not much was left except for some dismal-looking herons. When the marching men hove into sight, each heron cast a supercilious glance at them, then seemed to retreat into a brown study.

The Moor itself, burned off in a great fire before Otter's time, was hardly a moor any more. The forest was recapturing it, alder and rowan, birch and pine; but a clearing was kept open for the village, which nestled prettily, facing south over the lake and sheltered from the north wind by the young trees.

The march from the Meet to Swidden Moor had been a pleasant experience for Whitespear. He could not but be flattered by Chief Otter's interest in his company and in what he had to tell about life on the eastern seaboard. He even escaped being bored by Otter's predilection for old proverbs for the simple reason that he had not heard them before and took them to be witty and sagacious remarks. In addition, the successful hunt of an elk, during which the Chief imitated the roar of the bull moose to perfection, had revealed Otter as a first-rate hunter and leader of men.

There had been some awkward moments. As Whitespear realized, they were due to the fact that he had been born and reared among people with quite different ways of life. Tiger had warned him about this, but he had not foreseen all the possibilities. One such moment came when Whitespear spotted a bunch of chanterelles in the moss and innocently started to pick and eat them. He suddenly noticed that his companions had stopped and were staring at him, incredulity and awe in their faces. He stopped eating and looked from the yellow mushroom in his hand to the Chief.

"They are good," he said lamely.

Otter cleared his throat. Finally he said in a husky voice, "I did not realize you were a shaman, too, Whitespear."

Whitespear explained that mushrooms were eaten regularly by his people. Marveling, Otter remarked, "Then you must have powers that are denied to most of us. I am told that the shamans eat toadstools, and they come to know of things beyond mortal men. But to us they are death."

"Not these," Whitespear said. "Try one, Otter."

The Chief recoiled. He looked so terrified that Whitespear had to make an effort not to laugh. With that the incident was closed; musingly Otter repeated, "The horse eats the grass, but the stag eats the leaves," and left it at that. Yet for a day or two Whitespear was aware of the Chief's speculative gaze. For himself he resolved to be wary in the future, and to model his actions on those of Otter's men.

The incident led to many questions about the ways of the Trolls (as the Blacks called the Whites). Otter and his men listened with great interest and amusement, especially when Whitespear told of the power wielded by women among the Whites and about the style of White lovemaking, with the woman perched on top of the man. "Worth trying," said one of Otter's men, but Otter was skeptical. "Might put ideas in their heads," he said sagely.

Soon they were swapping stories, and again Whitespear found himself holding their attention. The Whites were great storytellers, and he knew many of their tales by heart. Some were horrifying, such as the one about the woman who exchanged her head and right hand for the head and forepaw of a hyena, became the leader of a hyena pack, and fed on human flesh and bones; in the end she was vanquished by a witch who was part woman, part lioness. There were also a lot of stories about a girl, most inappropriately called Rose Unblemished, who collected all manner of lovers, starting with very small ones the size of a hedgehog but rapidly progressing to the impossibly large—walking trees, mountains —and scattering the remarkable fruits of her unions at large. This amused Otter so much that he had to sit down while he rocked with laughter. "The Trolls must be a funny gang,

doing all these things," he said, wiping tears of laughter
from his eyes. "Oh, they don't do them," Whitespear explained. "They just tell the stories. They are really kind and
gentle." And he told how, many winters ago, the Whites
had nursed Tiger through a bad sickness and saved his life.
Otter thought for a while. Then his eyes lit up: "The bittern
booms like a bull, the serpent is silent and sly." He had
remembered a saving proverb.

They sang one of the Blacks' marching songs, a rousing
one all about the mishaps of a fool stalking the mammoth,
which ended with the unfortunate man falling into the mammoth trap; it had an endlessly repeated chorus and made
everybody merry. Otter asked Whitespear if the Trolls had
any songs, and Whitespear obligingly embarked upon a very
beautiful White song about stars and birds. Unlike the stories, it was not a success. Otter remarked that, with all due
respect, it reminded him more of the howling of wolves and
the laughter of hyenas than of a human song, and that he did
not think it would become popular with his men. Whitespear
grinned sheepishly and said that it might sound better if sung
by a White. Maybe, Otter granted, but he would rather not
risk it; there was already a raven cawing overhead and who
knew what other creatures might come running? The men
were still laughing and chaffing when they came in sight of
Horn Lake.

SISKIN

In the village a great feast was in preparation. The berry harvest had been plentiful, and some of the boys, too young to take part in the Meet, had succeeded in felling a big elk. Spirits were soaring. Whitespear was particularly enticed by the sight of so many Black girls: they all looked beautiful to him. Otter nudged him and said, "I will introduce you to the people."

The Chief jumped up on a boulder, lifted his spear, and called out. Leaving their work, the villagers thronged around him, looking expectant.

"My dear children," said Otter, "we have an honored guest. This is Whitespear. He comes from far away, from the great sea to the east. Look at him! He looks just like one of us: a tussock, or a resting hare"—a simile for two things indistinguishable—"and yet he is a man of great powers. He partakes of the wisdom of shamans. He tells wonderful tales of horror and laughter. He even sings the most unsonglike songs ever heard and has the knowledge of Trolls and witches. Above all, in his hands grow things of great beauty. We welcome him to Swidden Moor. He has come here to consult with our own beloved Shaman, Harrier, whose fame has spread to the ends of the world. So let us all rejoice and celebrate this occasion!"

There was a roar of eager applause, and Whitespear saw friendly, curious, and awed faces all around him. It went to his head, as if he had swallowed a big draught of black wine. Otter jumped down. "Where is Harrier the Shaman?" he asked.

There was a sudden awkward silence. Then somebody muttered from the back ranks, "We haven't seen him for a few days, Chief."

"He isn't here?" Otter said incredulously.

This was confirmed by various mumblings of "No, Chief." Otter was justifiably annoyed.

"Here I come and need the services of my Shaman, and what does the man do but fly off somewhere—only the hyena's Guardian knows where! Yes, Whitespear, you may kiss the hoofprint!" (Meaning "You are too late.") "I am not complaining," Otter went on in a rage. "No, I'm not! I am a patient man! I bear my burden all day without grumbling, like the snail who bears his house! You would think the man would have a sense of duty! Do we shirk when the mammoth hunt comes up, do we shirk when the berries ripen in the wood? No! But I keep my calm! It will not do for a chief to lose his temper and curse anybody, even if it is a damned good-for-nothing shaman who shirks his job," Otter finished piously.

"Why don't you turn him out and find another shaman?" ventured Whitespear.

Otter looked at him in surprise. "No, I couldn't do that. He is a good shaman, when he puts his mind to it. He was taught by Shelk himself. Why, he is the envy of every other tribe around here. I only hope that he hasn't decided to go to one of the other chiefs, such as Big Lake or Falcon Hill. That," Otter said, suddenly flying into another rage, "would be just like him, the damned traitor!" He started to dance around in his fury, but suddenly calmed down when a clear female voice called out:

"Father! Stop that! You have a guest!"

Whitespear spun around and saw the most beautiful girl he had ever seen. To be sure, he had seen only a few Black girls, and they all looked lovely to him, but this one shone out like a light. She was quite tall for a Black girl, she was exquisitely built, and she had the most glorious dark-brown eyes. Like most of the other girls she wore a short beaverskin dress which left her arms and legs bare, and in his mind he contrasted their slimness and grace with the robust limbs of the White women. Her black tresses were prettily coiled around her head. To Whitespear she was almost supernatural, and he fell in love on the spot.

He stared at her, his thoughts in a turmoil. He had completely forgotten his errand. Within him rose a tremendous conviction that he wanted her more than anything else in the world. But she was the daughter of a chief. What a hope! Could he ever make good enough to cajole Otter into giving her to him? For Whitespear knew well, from Tiger's and Hind's stories, what was required by a suitor among the Blacks.

Otter and the girl walked away. She was holding his hand, and the Chief went meekly enough, docile after his outburst. Whitespear stared after them. One of Otter's men looked searchingly at him, then smiled. "Good-looking wench, isn't she?" he observed.

"Who is she?"

"She is Siskin, the Chief's daughter. He thinks a lot of her." The man seemed on the verge of adding something. Finally he went on: "The Chief has a son, but he has moved

away. He lives at Falcon Hill now. Like the mammoth and
the rhinoceros they were: they didn't get along." Whitespear
had the impression that the man had originally intended to
say something else but had changed his mind.

"She is beautiful," Whitespear said, trying to sound non-
committal.

"That she is," the man agreed. "Can I interest you in a
drop of wine?" He produced a skin, and they both drank.
The man had a trick of holding the skin high above his head
and spurting a jet into his open mouth. The wine, which
looked black in the horn, now revealed its true color in the
sunshine: it coursed through the air like a purple-red flame.
Whitespear felt its cool glow within him and was surprised
at his lightheadedness. The man still hesitated, then smiled
again. "See you later," he said and was gone. A couple of
girls, giggling excitedly, spoke to Whitespear. He answered
politely but was unable afterward to remember what they
had talked about. Suddenly the girls, still giggling, ran away.
Whitespear felt a hand on his arm and turned to look into
Siskin's radiant eyes.

"Whitespear," she said in her clear voice. "A powerful
name. My father has told me about you. He wants me to tell
you that you are welcome to stay with us until the Shaman
comes back, and as long after that as you wish. He would be
honored to have you stay under his roof. You will do that,
won't you?"

Finding his voice, Whitespear answered, "The honor is on
my side."

.   .   .

Autumn and winter had passed. The promise of spring was
in the air. It was a mild and foggy day, and Whitespear was
slowly trudging south. He had been away from Swidden
Moor for almost a whole moon, and he would rather have

stayed longer. In a somber mood, he reluctantly tramped through the fog-swept forest, following a game path in the slushy snow. He was wet through, but more than the weather, his own thoughts burdened him.

Ruefully he thought back on his time with Chief Otter's people. It had started so well. He remembered that first evening alone with the enchanting Siskin in her father's house. He had been at her side during the feast, adoring the way in which she ate her venison: she would take a piece of meat between her white teeth and cut it off with a small flint knife, giving him a sidelong look into which he read a promise. She had donned finery that surpassed anything he had seen. On her forehead she wore the shell of a pearl mussel, fashioned into a round disk like the Sun-mark of a shamaness, and glittering in the hues of the rainbow; it was held in place by a headband. Whitespear had heard of the big river mussels and of the pearls that were occasionally found in them, tears of some sad Guardian of the deeps, but he had never seen them. Even grander, though, was the amber jewel on her breast. He could not resist bending over to have a close look. In the amber floated a wasp as if alive. This was marvelous —the sheen of the amber, collecting the sun's rays, against her brown skin, and that silent wasp stilled forever in its golden prison. "I put them on in your honor," she whispered. She fingered the amber pendant and smiled. "This wasp belonged to a friend of my father. He was Wolf, a great chief, who died many years ago."

"I wish I could fashion things like these," said Whitespear admiringly.

"But you can," said Siskin. "My father tells me that you are a great artist, that you were taught by Tiger himself, the greatest master of all. Among all the things in my father's house, there is nothing to compare with the drinking-horn made by Tiger."

"My handiwork cannot compete with your gems."

"But they were not made by man: they come from the hands of the Guardians."

She was right, and Whitespear, greatly encouraged, thought he knew now how to press his suit. They went on eating and drinking, chatting pleasantly. The sun was close to the edge of the forest when Siskin stretched her arms in the air, gave a delicate but approving burp, and told him she was full. Whitespear, who had eaten sparingly but had a good hornful of wine inside him, rose with her, and they strolled away.

Inside Otter's house, he was momentarily taken aback. The place contained a veritable hoard of valuables, ranging from flintwork to carved bone and antler utensils. A look at the latter, however, reassured him. The work was crude for the most part: he could do better.

Before her eager eyes, he unpacked his precious bundle. He smiled proudly at her excited cries. Oh yes, it was all hers! He wanted to show that he was worthy of her. The beautiful pendant with its carved bear's head, the bone comb, the necklace of seal teeth, the magical bull-roarer—it was all for her. The other things would be for Otter, a bride's princely ransom. The spear-spokeshave made from an elk antler, the carefully bored hole so cleverly forming the eye of a bison. His special pride, the exquisitely ornamented spear-thrower made from a reindeer antler specially selected for its closely angled tine. Yes, he had thought it all out. And would she have him? He could do more. He had visions of beautiful things taking shape in his hands. Would she? Yes, yes! She could hardly stop admiring the treasures, but soon she was in his arms.

And then all went wrong. He felt his cheeks burn when he thought of that first embrace.

He only knew love White fashion, the woman riding her man. But Siskin expected *him* to ride *her,* and the memory of the ensuing confusion made him groan aloud. Unsettled and bewildered, he had become completely incompetent and was crouching miserably beside Siskin, both of them stark naked, when Otter walked in.

Alone in the forest, Whitespear stopped in his tracks. Picture after picture rose before his inner eye, and he waved his hands vigorously in a futile attempt to drive them away. There was Otter, very polite, very understanding, looking fixedly at a point somewhere above Whitespear's head, clearly at great pains to suppress a grin, and bringing out a string of adages about Young Blood and the Mating Season, and the prowess of the Bison Bull who mightily penetrates his Beautiful and Willing Cow, and the Chief of the Wolves choosing his Mistress and impregnating her under the eyes of the Faithful Pack, and how New Hunters and Mothers would strengthen the ranks of the Swidden Moor people in summers to come. There was Siskin, her limpid eyes unfathomable, betraying nothing, but she knew, and he knew, what had happened and what had not. And then the exquisitely irritating feeling of his manhood rising, and knowing that now, NOW, he could have done what he wanted to do with her if only that proverb-spouting Chief would remove himself. Clumsily getting dressed, trying to cover up that insolent part of him which so clearly proclaimed what had not happened. Then felicitations from a crowd of people collected outside the Chief's house, and another great impromptu speech by Otter, reiterating everything, Bull Bison, Wolf Chief, Mating Season, Young Blood, and various other things for good measure, including Whitespear's shamanistic powers and skilled hands, and even the tussock and the resting hare, all of which Whitespear listened to fuming with inward anger.

Out here in the fog with ghostly tree-trunks all around, Whitespear was suddenly struck by the absurdity of it all. He leaned on a tree and burst into a tormented laugh. Soon he was laughing freely, and those ghosts at least took flight. What he had thought his own design was in reality that of Otter and Siskin. They had wanted him.

Well, at least the anger had been timely: that night he took her three times, Black fashion. The memory of that was comforting.

.   .   .

The fog seemed to be less dense in this part of the forest. Maybe it would lift soon. Was he headed the right way? He looked at the trees and felt reassured: he was still going south, by and large, even though there was no sun to guide him. He felt a sudden urge to get back to Swidden Moor. Maybe Harrier had turned up there while he was away!

Harrier: that was his trouble. He ought to have tried harder to find him. He had been content to stay with Siskin. No, not content: he had been pulled two ways all the time. The thought of Baywillow, of his life on Veyde's Island, belonged somehow to another world, yet there was the pull.

Well, he told himself, I've tried. In the autumn, before the heavy snowfalls, he had made a journey south to Falcon Hill, much to Siskin's annoyance, in the hope of gathering some news of the wayward shaman. It had been an effort to tear himself away from his lovely bride, and all to no avail: Harrier wasn't there, and nobody knew where he was. He had met Otter's son Hedgehog, a young man his own age, who had grinned and wished him luck when he heard White-spear's story.

After that, the snow had come very thick, which made it difficult to move about: long journeys were out of the question. He had built a house for Siskin and himself and spent the winter at Swidden Moor. But now he was returning from a trip to Big Lake in the northeast—and once more he was coming back with his errand unaccomplished.

Harrier had not been at Big Lake. More than that, there had been nobody there at all. At first, he thought he had come to the wrong place. But everything tallied with the descriptions he had heard, and the village was there—only there were no people. Some of the houses had caved in under their burden of snow, but otherwise it looked just as if the people had left for a day or so, expecting to come back at any moment. He went from house to house. Hunting utensils, skins and rugs, household things, toys, even some frozen food, it was all there; only the fires had burned out.

He walked about as in a dream. Everything was in place, seeming confidently to expect the return of the villagers. He shouted, but nobody answered.

What had happened? Had they all been killed by a plague? No: there would be human remains about. For some unfathomable reason, all the people of Big Lake had suddenly got up and gone he could not imagine where, leaving all their things behind. He looked for footprints, in the village or leading out of it, but there were only some animal prints; that meant they had left long ago. Had some mysterious power scooped them up into the sky?

Perhaps, he thought, the place had come under a spell. Perhaps they had offended a powerful Guardian in such a way that their Chief or Shaman had to tell them they must go away and start anew in some other place. Maybe all these things were still under a spell. Well, he hoped the Guardian would not mind his visit. He had done no harm, and he would leave everything as he had found it.

He thought of spending the night in one of the houses. He looked into one and saw a half-finished garment lying on the floor. At the sight he backed out. No, he would not sleep in the village.

In his temporary lair outside the village, he slept badly nonetheless, oppressed by a vague feeling of menace. In the morning he forced himself to go back for a last look. Nothing had changed. He felt relieved when he turned his back on Big Lake.

His problem remained unsolved. He had not found Harrier, and he had to find him. He thought it over. If the shaman had been at Big Lake, he presumably had left with

the others. Maybe he had even led them away. But there was
nothing to show that Harrier had been there. What ought
he, Whitespear, to do now? Should he try to find another
helper? All his instincts told him to hold on to the idea of
Harrier, and that meant going back to Swidden Moor, first
of all.

Back to Siskin. Now, in the misty forest, his thoughts
returned to her. That great laugh had cleared his mind and
made him able to think about himself and her less personally,
less haunted by emotions than before. Something had been
wrong, but he didn't know what. They had quarreled a great
deal, but surely that was not his fault? She was at her happiest
when he worked, when he fashioned beautiful things for her,
and he had been doing a good many—very happily, too.
After a day of that she would be warm and open to him, and
they would make love in their new house. On the other
hand, if he went out hunting with the other men, she would
be preoccupied and uninterested and go to sleep with her
back turned. She had long spells of irritability when she
flared out at him for no reason he could understand.

Even at her best she never seemed to find the kind of
abandonment in her lovemaking that came so easily to him.
Sometimes he found himself remembering Marigold, big
and fat and shining, ablaze with her passion, crying out as it
shook her. "How different they are!" he mused aloud. "It
cannot be my fault. I am the same to both of them." But
while Siskin remained cool and passive, he still was deeply
moved by her beauty and her delicate ways. After all these
moons she still seemed almost supernatural to him. To see
her was to drink her in, with pictures forming in his mind,
pictures crying out to be revealed, to take shape under his
hands.

To him she was beautiful even in her anger. Once she had
berated him for leaving a work unfinished to go out hunting
a bear that had slain a woman returning from the cranberry
bog. He told her the bear would always be a danger, and

that they had to find it, though it took them three days; but
she would not listen. Yet while she was scolding him, his
eyes followed the taut, ever-changing lines of her body and
arms, and there was such glory in them that he suddenly got
to his feet, gathered her up, and kissed her stormily. She was
taken aback; in the end she said, "I was frightened for you.
Oh, that bear might have bitten off your hand!" He laughed
at that, and soon she laughed too, and they were reconciled.

The fog was clearing. He could see a long way ahead now.
There was open ground in front of him. Why, the sun was
breaking through! He felt a sudden joy, as if some wonderful
experience awaited him out there in the glade.

· · ·

She was crouching just inside the door. The fog had lifted
and there was a pool of sunshine on the earthen floor. A little
while ago, shaken by nausea, she had fled behind the house
to vomit. The sickness passed quickly and she felt empty and
cleansed, free and thoughtless. She was sitting in the shade,
but her open hand was in the sunlight and in it there shone a
pearl.

It met her gaze like a smiling eye. She could hardly remember how she had got it, or when. Yesterday? Some day.
Now it smiled at her. It was hers. Her eyes widened to take
in its radiance like a whispered secret.

Who was it that lived in the pearl, that smiled at her in
there? It was not a tear fallen in sorrow. A Guardian of the
deeps had wept for joy and part of his spirit had entered into
this thing which now rested in her outstretched hand. It was
a charmed thing: a spirit effulgent with joy. It would remain
with her always, and with the child she was now expecting,
and with coming generations. A great horizon seemed to
open in front of her and she saw a train of people moving
towards the future. That train had emanated from herself,
maybe she was one of them, walking towards the sun and

the warmth. Vehemently she pressed the pearl to her breast and thought she felt the glow of its spirit.

The nausea returned briefly and brought a reminder of the man, but only to give her a passing feeling of contempt. What a fool he was! He did not understand. It was not right for him to have such a treasure. She knew at once, when she saw it, that it was hers. Yet she had not cheated him. No, she had paid for it. Paid! She laughed. It had cost her nothing. Already she carried the child, hers and Whitespear's. The other thing had nothing to do with her. For a moment she wondered whether Otter knew. That did not matter. All that mattered now were the pearl, the child, herself. And somewhere just outside, still half-seen in the dark, the returning father and artist with his powerful name. She tried to remember him and found it difficult. She tried hard: she made herself light and kind, smiling and graceful. Still, like a cloud over her thoughts, there hovered another picture, of herself supine, flat on her back, legs spread out, the pearl clutched in her hand, the puffing man laboring on top of her. But the cloud dispersed when she met the unblemished gaze of the pearl. All was lightness, innocence, joy. Now she could permit Whitespear to enter her picture. He was still a figure without a face.

She gave a start. The figure had eyes, and they looked sharply at her. At once she rose, drove the vision of Whitespear away, and began to move about uneasily in the house that he had built. She fingered various things, beautiful things that he had made. She wanted to embellish herself: she handled the ornaments, held them at arm's length, made a thoughtful face, spoke in a low voice. She wanted to go down to the water and look at her reflection. Then she put the things back, irresolutely. All the time she clutched the pearl in her hand, feeling its consoling warmth.

In the end she started to scrape the skin of a beaver that Otter had snared. The scraper was flintwork from the South. She did not remember how she had got it.

She scraped violently, almost tore a hole in the skin, and checked herself. Enough: now she must chew it. While her jaws worked, a new wave of nausea swept her and brought another picture. Again she saw a train of people, but these were all men and they were approaching her. They were faceless, too, but in their outstretched hands they carried many things, treasures of amber and mother-of-pearl, carved ivory, noble flintwork. The men were just a pack of grey figures; she could not remember a single one. Oh yes, one, the first one: she remembered him for his hands, always fluttering, but she could not give him a name. She looked at them coldly. They rated nothing but her contempt. She was cleverer than they. She had everything. They had nothing, nothing—only a pale memory, perhaps.

Through winters and summers she looked back at her past life and was a child again with her mother, her mother dead long ago. "You are a chief's daughter," said her mother, "you will be a chief's woman. He will be the greatest hunter under the Sun, he will be big, strong, and tender, he will give you mother-of-pearl and amber, ivory and wolverine skins.

"*That* you should do: that behooves a chief's daughter.

"*That* you must not do: that does not behoove a chief's daughter."

Siskin was intelligent and quick at learning. Soon she knew what behooves a chief's daughter.

A chief's daughter should outshine all others in beauty. And she did. Her reflection in the clear water of Horn Lake told her that, and so did the whispered compliments of the old women and men to her parents: "What a remarkably beautiful child!"

A chief's daughter should adorn herself with exquisite things. And she did. Her father presented her with costly gifts, and soon she found other ways to increase her treasures, when traders rested at Swidden Moor.

A chief's daughter should become the bride of a great

man. And she did. None of the local youngsters would do, but now she had the greatest artist in the land for a husband.

At the thought of Whitespear she felt warmth and longing. She saw herself running to meet him, crying out her secret: a child!

The pearl in her open hand glowed as if burning with love. It was hers forever. They had a compact, she and the spirit of the pearl.

For the last time she had a fleeting memory of its former owner, and she pitied him. He had nothing left—nothing.

Thus wretchedly did she underestimate herself and that which she had given him.

 HARRIER

Whitespear told Oriole:
"That was the first time I saw Singletusk: on my
return from Big Lake. I knew then it was a sign of luck, and
from that day there was a compact between us, Singletusk
and me. He frightened me just a little, that first time, when
I saw him in his strength and his weakness. But I was to
learn that he was an omen of good things to come; and he
never deceived me.

"I had been tramping on since dawn. The last days had
been foggy and dismal, and there was little to eat besides last
year's lingonberries. They are sweet, but they don't make a
bellyful.

"For a moon or more, mammoth herds had been passing
by, going north. He didn't care for herds, though, not he! A

loner, that's what he was. He had been up to some mischief in the South, I bet.

"The mist was gone, and all seemed to change. The sun felt warm. My path took me through scattered stands of pines out onto a heath with low rounded knolls and a few small trees. The lichen was thick and soft, and I sat down with the sun in my face and a tree at my back. It felt good. While I sat there basking and drying, everything around me seemed to come awake. In the tree overhead a couple of greenfinches started to sing their *tuu-ee,* repeating themselves endlessly. No other bird speaks with such stubborn conviction. He seems to be telling you the most important thing in the world, and he says it over and over again, in case you forget.

"Then I saw him in front of me. He was going north all by himself. I could see him far away, in among the trees at the forest's edge. In there he was little more than a black shadow, but his tusk shone out boldly in the dark wood. Then he came out on the heath.

"He was going along at a trot, gliding and springy, as if he had been no heavier than a roebuck. He lifted his feet very high and put them down again very delicately, *so-so-so-so, one-two-three-four, one-two-three-four.* You could see the muscles rippling under his skin as if dancing to a tune. He was silent as a cloud, but you felt he surged forward to the roll of tomtoms and the song of flutes. Oh, he was the biggest, the strongest, the proudest in the world! That flashing black body, from the two fingers at the tip of his trunk to the whisk of his tail. Every single hair, even the glitter of sunshine that enveloped his power and glory: it all belonged to him. He owned the world as far as he could see—and he was long-sighted like all mammoths. I saw his eye, and in it gleamed the cool assurance of the all-powerful.

"No, he didn't see me. I was too small, and too close. But he took in all the most distant things, and they were his property: the edge of the forest, the rising hills to the north, the kite in the sky. He was perfect and he knew it. I never saw a more conceited mammoth.

"Of course, he wasn't really perfect, for he had only one tusk. The other had been broken; I could see the stump protruding a handsbreadth out of his mouth. The left tusk was entire, and it was the biggest I have ever seen. It emerged from his jaw and curved outward, then forward, and finally inward, so that its point was turned to the right. Yes, he carried a spear, pointing to the right, more than a man's length in front of him! A spear, but also a snowplow and a battering-ram, all rolled into one. Oh, he was a black cloud and his tusk a flash of lightning.

"I had been looking for game, but this was game beyond me. I just kept still, and he didn't see me. As he came closer, he loomed ever bigger. At the same time—I can't describe it, but a tremendous change seemed to come over him. The arrogance, which was the first thing that had struck me about him, seemed to fall off him like a cloak. He was dig-nified as a chief—awesome, but not old: there was power, youth, lightness about him. Maybe it was the dainty way he lifted his feet—I don't know.

"Now he was so close to me that he would have picked up my scent if the wind had been that way. But what little wind there was blew from him to me, so I could smell him. His scent was that of the lonely rogue.

"And then the grouse flew up.

"He had almost trodden on her as she hid in the lichen, and she shot up right in his face with a tremendous whirring and a scream—*Go back!*

"By all the Guardians, what a fright it gave him! He reared up on his hind legs, his trunk went high, his ears flapped out, and he all but fell over backward. His hair stood on end, yet he seemed to shrink together. I expected him to topple with a crash, but he thumped down on all fours and started to look around, trying to catch sight of whatever hideous danger he'd stumbled on. His single tusk wobbled and swept about with his movements.

"Then slowly he realized that it was nothing dangerous. I could see him sort of freeze and become quite still. His hair gradually came back to normal, his ears turned back, and his trunk went down. He looked so silly that I dug my fingers into my thighs to keep myself from laughing.

"Now he moved stiffly, turning a little to one side and then the other. I could see his eye again, and it was uneasy: had anybody seen him make a fool of himself? Had he noticed me, he'd have murdered me out of hurt pride.

"He didn't see me. The greenfinches were silent. Nothing moved. He seemed to swell up again, and I can swear I read relief in his eye: no, nobody had seen him. Hah. H'm. Why, it was just a grouse. Nothing to worry about. Could happen to anybody. Oh, I could read his mind, all right! Of course he hadn't been frightened, not really. Just a bit of horseplay. You do this for fun—eh?

"He took a couple of steps forward. All was silent. Then why all that uproar? Now his eye was angry: can't a peaceful mammoth walk across a heath without these odious birds banging about?

"He thought it over, and his eye became peaceful. Never mind, let's forget it. I'm the Chief. I'm even-tempered. And within a few breaths he was moving again, a little hesitantly at first, then with increasing confidence. He passed me unheeding, and when he vanished in the woods he was loping along as lightly as ever, lifting his feet high, *one-two-three-four, one-two-three-four.*"

. . .

Whitespear woke up with a start. He had been asleep with his back against the tree. He started to rise, but checked himself at the sight of three men coming over the moor just like Singletusk earlier in the day. He recalled Otter's stories about wolfmen and outcasts, and scrutinized them suspiciously. They carried heavy packs and moved slowly. One of them walked with a bad limp. They don't look dangerous, he told himself, and got up.

The men made the open-hand peace sign from afar, and Whitespear did the same.

They were traders. The spokesman, a tall fellow with the red shaman symbol on his forehead, told him that they came from the Salt Sea. They had wonderful things from the coast, he said: sealskins and shells, firestones and whale teeth. He put down his pack, and Whitespear saw that what he had taken for a long javelin was in fact a kind of pointed scepter, oddly twisted its whole length. Noting his curious glance, the man smiled. "It's the horn of a sea-ox," he said. "It sits on the brow of the ox and points straight forward. Sea-oxen have only one horn—though I've heard a story about one that had two."

The men had a good supply of dried meat, and hearing that Whitespear was hungry, they asked him to share their meal.

Their real objective, as it turned out, was a pilgrimage. The spokesman, whose name was Greyseal, and his brother, who was only called Lamey, wanted to journey to Caribou Lake in the far North. Their father, whose name was Horned Owl, had been the leader of a group of men there long ago, under the legendary Shelk. Such stories as he had told them about those times! Now that he was dead, they wanted to see the place for themselves. The third traveler was a youngster who had joined them out of sheer love of adventure. They were well equipped with trading goods.

The youngster was shy and taciturn, and Lamey, too, seemed to have few words. He was unshapely, with a crooked back and a short leg. He looked up humbly at his tall brother. "He got his injuries as a boy," Greyseal explained. "He's not too bright, but there is no evil in him."

Lamey, in fact, had a mildly happy look in spite of his deformity.

"You have nothing to trade, I can see that," said Greyseal. "Still, we can give you a seashell to remember us by."

Whitespear looked admiringly at the treasures in Greyseal's pack. Greyseal laughed. "Yes, but Lamey has the greatest treasure of us all. Show it, Brother."

Lamey shook his head. "Haven't got it any more," he said.

"Have you lost it?" cried Greyseal.

"Gave it away."

"Without payment? To whom?"

"Got paid. She was the loveliest of them all."

"You gave your pearl to a woman and she paid you by letting you sleep with her?"

Lamey nodded happily. "The loveliest," he repeated.

Greyseal burst into a laugh. "You are a fool! All of last summer he spends diving in the river for mussels. In the end he finds a pearl. And he gives it away for an embrace!"

Lamey looked peacefully at his brother. "Never did a woman look at me twice," he said. "They laugh and point their fingers. At Crooky. At Lamey. If I'd been an artist, then maybe . . . But I have no skill. And then I found the pearl. Then I thought that maybe . . . I'd save it for the loveliest. And I was right."

He smiled, animated by the memory.

Still laughing, Greyseal chaffed him: "The Great River runs out of Caribou Lake. Do you plan to find another pearl there?"

Lamey nodded. "New pearl. For the loveliest."

"And if you don't get it?"

"Doesn't matter. I still remember. Remember it all."

He looked shyly at Whitespear. "It was the first time. Didn't know what it was like. Now I know. Never forget."

Whitespear felt strangely moved. This humble, crooked-grown man who didn't even have a name of his own had

traded a treasure for a brief moment of love, and thought it
a bargain. Maybe he was right. Maybe he was wiser than
other men.

They separated, embracing and wishing each other luck.

.   .   .

A third encounter awaited Whitespear on that day. Once
more he came out into a glade with moss-covered rocks, and
there he spied a small walking figure. Why, it's a girl! he said
aloud. And just a child!

The girl stopped at the sight of him. He made the peace
sign and came on with raised palms. He called out from afar
and told her his name. She did not answer, but remained
standing, following him with her eyes.

"I have seen you in Horn Lake Village, haven't I?" said
Whitespear, who now thought he recognized her face. She
was bundled up in skin rags, with a hood about her head,
and her face had a grimy look. She staggered a little, as if
tired.

"Got any food?" she asked. Her voice was deep and
hoarse, and he realized that she was a grown woman after
all. He put down his pack. Greyseal had given him some
dried meat, but here was somebody who needed it more than
he. The girl sat down and started to wolf down the food.
Whitespear looked closely at her. Yes, he had seen her in the
village, but only at the very end, the day before he left for
Big Lake. He did not know whether she belonged to the
people of Swidden Moor—he had not asked. Still, he remembered her face. She had studied him from a distance; her
gaze had swept him until she met his eyes, then she had
looked away. "I saw you in the village," he said. "Just before
I went away. What's your name?"

She looked at him from beneath her tousled fringe. "I
know you," she said. "You're Siskin's latest." She laughed,
a peculiar panting laugh almost like a hiccough, and it flashed

through Whitespear's mind that he had heard that laughter before. That was how his mother Hind used to laugh.

She went on eating, and he looked at her in silence. She took her time. She removed a skin from her belt, drank, and went on eating. Suddenly aware of his gaze, she looked up with a grin and handed him the skin. "Thanks for the food."

Whitespear drank. He expected it to be water, but it was wine, a pungent wine with a peculiar taste, and he almost choked. The girl took off her hood and pushed her hair back, and he saw the shaman symbol on her forehead. "You have partaken of the wine of the shamans, Whitespear," she said. "May it give you strength."

"So you're a shaman! But you haven't told me your name."

She still had a piece of meat left. At last she was finished and licked her fingertips. Her cool eyes passed over him, as if measuring him. "My name is Kite," she said, "daughter of Harrier, greatest of shamans."

Surprise, and perhaps the wine too, made Whitespear's head swirl. His knees buckled and he sat down. He took her hands.

"Then I have found what I have looked for so long! Can you take me to Harrier?"

"Why should I?"

She now looked straight into his eyes, and he felt dizzier than ever. Was it something else, something more powerful than wine—or was it the power of her eyes? At once she seemed far away: he was still holding her hands, yet she was immeasurably distant, and her voice reached him as if from across the sea.

"You have quaffed the wine of the shamans." Then her voice changed: *"Now you are ours: our man, our fire, our spear: to command, to kindle, to throw."*

Whitespear blinked and shook his head. The girl was close to him again, and he was filled with wrath.

"You are wrong," he said vehemently, and in the same breath he realized that she had spoken to him *in the tongue of the Whites* and that he had answered in the same language. "Stop it! Your witchcraft does not work on me."

At the sight of Kite's face he ceased speaking. Her mouth fell open in ludicrous astonishment. Then she burst into a laugh. She put her hands before her face and rocked back and forth, helpless with mirth. Whitespear had to smile.

"Oh," groaned Kite at last, "you must think the hyena got my tongue. But I didn't know—oh, ha-ha!—I did not know that you were one of us. You speak the secret language of the shamans! I feel so embarrassed!"

"It is the White tongue you speak," said Whitespear, "though you get it wrong sometimes."

"To us it is the language of the shamans. My father learned it from Shelk himself, and then he gave it to me. It goes from generation to generation among the shamans."

Her mocking manners were gone and she looked kindly at Whitespear. "And why do you wish to see Harrier? Is it for the sake of your woman?"

"Siskin?" said Whitespear, surprised. "No, why? It is for the sake of my father Baywillow that I wish to talk to Harrier. No one can help us unless he can, that is my belief."

And he told her about Baywillow. But Kite interrupted him before long and said, "Let us go. Harrier shall hear your story: I am taking you to him."

. . .

They were working their way up a slope, all overgrown with brush and covered by patches of treacherous, melting ice, when they suddenly heard heavy trampling and panting. In the next breath, something big came crashing down: a panicked heifer elk, tumbling through the brushes in a confusion of long legs and broken branches. In a single leap

Whitespear was upon her, his spear went through her heart, and the animal died, still sliding down the slope.

"Good hunting gave Singletusk," said Whitespear, pulling out his spear. "She was wounded, though." He pointed at another spear in the elk's shoulder.

Kite looked close, then grinned impishly. "The old man is really getting old," she said. "He won't be in his best mood right now."

She gave a hunting yell, which was answered from afar.

"Now, Whitespear, you will meet Harrier. I hope he is hungry enough to forget that it wasn't his spear that killed the elk."

"Not far from it," remarked Whitespear, who had been studying the animal. "She broke a leg when she fell down. He'd have got her without our help."

Kite laughed, that peculiar laugh which touched his heart in such an odd way. "He is going to like that piece of news."

.   .   .

Kite was right. Harrier arrived in a very surly mood but was visibly mollified when he was told what had happened. He was a small, thin man with a straight back like a spear, a face that seemed to express a perpetual grievance, and roving eyes. His speech was brief and abrupt, but sometimes he broke into long tirades, usually in the White tongue. Then he would cross his arms and stand with his head thrown back, as if listening to the whisperings of a spirit.

His first words to Kite consisted of a gruff question, in the White language, concerning Whitespear. Kite, with a mischievous glint in her eye, told him that he was Otter's daughter's man. Harrier frowned ominously.

"Otter!" he spat out, still in the White tongue. "That Guardian of the woodlouse! The man whose words are like so many farts. To say nothing of his precious daughter—"

He was interrupted by Kite, who sweetly observed, "Mister Whitespear speaks the shaman language." This struck Harrier dumb, and Kite went on to tell about the hunting of the elk. Harrier listened, arms akimbo.

"Tchaa!" he said at last. "Oh, so we speak the secret tongue, do we?"

"Mister Harrier, you speak the White language just like a White," said Whitespear, politely if not entirely truthfully, and a faint smile passed over the shaman's face. "Tchaa! Well, well. We seem to speak it quite well."

"Father, the time has come for you to give Otter the sign of the open hand," said Kite. "I have talked to the people of Horn Lake Village. They all want you back, and so does Otter."

"That pisser into the wind! That half-assed dotard!"

"You want back home yourself. Besides, you shouldn't go on living in the forest and teaching our secrets to anybody who comes here and flatters you."

Harrier crossed his arms and gave his daughter a murderous glance. "Tchaa!" he said, outraged. "Anybody? That was no anybody, that wasn't. She was a clever one."

"Yes, and she spread her legs for you."

"Tchaa! Tchaa! That is none of your business. She spoke the Language."

"And you gave her our wine. The wine that lets us see the spirits and Guardians and talk with them."

Harrier scratched his nose. He appeared somewhat embarrassed. "Well, well," he murmured. "She was a pretty one, and clever in her head and in her loins too. And it is so long ago! In the autumn that was, Kite, and you were out collecting the red mushrooms—"

"And you taught her how to use them."

"She spoke the Language," insisted Harrier. "And she had the makings of a great shaman. And—do you know?—she reminded me of Shelk himself. I think he would understand and forgive me for saying so, for indeed there was a resemblance. Yes, she had the same eyes, the same brow, the same bearing. Yes, that was no anybody."

Kite laughed. "Let it pass, Father dear. Let us eat. Look at Whitespear!"

While they were bickering, Whitespear had collected firewood and lit a fire, using the firestone, flint, and tinder that he carried in a pouch. He had listened to Harrier and Kite's talk but without realizing its significance, and it was much later that he understood that they had been talking about Avens. Now the elk tongue was on the fire. The smell was pleasing, and Harrier suddenly smiled a big grin, which transformed his face.

"Tchaa! We'll think about it. You are a good daughter, Kite. It may be that you are right. Otter has learned his lesson. I shall enter Horn Lake Village again!"

Harrier and Kite had something to discuss during the meal. Whitespear knew that it concerned him, for every now and then the old shaman would cast a thoughtful glance at him. At first the girl did most of the talking, and Whitespear thought that she was trying to persuade her father. Soon it was the other way around, though: Harrier spoke at length with impatient gestures, while Kite looked troubled. Once she even rose and made a gesture of despair. In the end they appeared to agree. The shaman took a pull at the wineskin, and Kite cogitated for a while.

Then she rose with an air of decision and crossed over to the young hunter.

"My father bids you welcome," she said. "He says that you have the makings of a shaman, because you speak the Language. And he says that we are going to help you. Yet his lot is to go back to Swidden Moor, and mine is to go with you to Veyde's Island. It will be my first great task, and the thought makes me tremble. So we must go to the Sanctuary where I can draw upon the Powers. You are not an initiate yet, so I shall have to lead you, blindfolded, so as not to betray the road there. Such is the law and such is the oath that the disciples took at Shelk's body, winters ago. If you break it, the Powers will break you, and you will lose the light of your eyes."

SHELK

The anthill was the first thing he saw when they took off the blindfold. He was on his knees in the moss, and it loomed up like a mountain in front of him at the edge of a little glade. Dark and mysteriously potent, it was bigger than anything he had seen before. It was asleep, without a sign of life, but the straight roads of the ants radiated in all directions across the moss-clad rock. In their dense myriads they had worn away the moss and lichen so that the grey rock shone through in the evening light. There was something terrifying about that anthill. He had never bothered about ants: they were small, crawling things you stepped on, and their bite was just a tickle. Yet the enormousness of this silent anthill made it strange and terrible, as if its inhabitants might suddenly surge out and flood everything in a mass of crawling, rustling, living matter.

The old Shaman, kneeling beside Whitespear, put his hands before his eyes in a quick gesture that Whitespear recognized as the greeting of the Whites. His nostrils were dilated, as if to catch the scent that would forebode the awakening of the nest.

"This is where Shelk is," he said quietly. Whitespear looked wonderingly at him: "Shelk?" he repeated, puzzled.

The Shaman rose and made a sign to Kite and Whitespear to follow him. Whitespear looked again at the anthill: even when he stood up it rose above his head, tall as a resting mammoth. Harrier led them away, moving stiffly and solemnly, with his hands pressed to his breast. Before the wood closed about him, Whitespear stopped for a final look at the place sacred to Shelk, and this time it became a picture in his inner eye. It flowed into him and filled him to the brim, never to be forgotten: the resting giant and behind it—as he now saw—white-stemmed birches like strange symbols carved on the black background of the forest. The biggest birch, a chief among youngsters, was proud and straight like a white spear. A white spear! The pictures merged, separated, and merged again: Singletusk, the Guardian he had seen as a child, his own name. And into that picture there gathered all the strange figures he had met in his wanderings: Goshawk, toothless and mumbling; Siskin, enigmatic and alluring; Avens, lying in the ring of mushrooms; courteous Helleborine, incredibly spitting in the face of a dead man; the flint-dealer with his fluttering hands; Lamey, humble in his happiness; Harrier—

Kite touched his hand. "What is it you see, Whitespear?"

"A picture."

It was all he could say, but as he uttered the words, the picture became clear to his inner eye, as if seen in the mirror of a pool stilled after a gust of wind; and he knew that it had to be shaped by his hand.

. . .

Harrier's hut lay on the other side of a copse. Kite revived
the fire that had been sleeping under its cover of wet moss.
She brought fuel to feed it, but her eyes, flickering in the
firelight, were on her father and their guest. Whitespear,
who had cleaned the shoulder blade of the elk, sat down with
his engraving tool to work on the picture that he carried
within him and that would give him no peace until it was
finished.

Harrier was speaking. He spoke contemplatively, without
his usual mannerisms:

"Of all masters, Shelk was the greatest. He was more than
a man: he was a ruler of Trolls and men. The caribou were
his cattle, received from his father the Sun. The two others
of the Sun's cattle are the mammoth and the shelk, and they
are all wanderers, moving as the Sun bids them. Caribou and
mammoth move towards the North Star, but the shelk mi-
grates south and escapes the cold in the Land of Flints. Of
these three, Shelk received the caribou, the humblest one,
and his father the Sun retained the proud ones."

Dusk was falling. A horned owl called, and the fire seemed
to burn with a stronger light. In the trees hung the moon,
red and gibbous.

"He stretched out his hand, and the birds of the sky
perched on it and hailed him as their master and the Son of
the Sun. I, Harrier from the Three Rapids, have seen it with
my own eyes. Thus he gained power over the Trolls and
made their wisdom his own.

"Everything, everything I learned from him! He had no
sons of his own, but we, his disciples, were like sons to him,
and in us his powers are still alive. We were four: Harrier
from the Three Rapids, Boar from the Land of Flints, Eagle
from the Hill, and Whitebear from the shore of the Salt Sea.
And amongst us, I was the foremost and the closest to him.

Yet we were like small children in his arms. Thus say I, Harrier, greatest of shamans in a shrinking world: within me lives the waxing shade of Shelk, yet it is but a shade and will remain so."

He sighed and took a pull at the wineskin.

"All who were stricken by the spirits sought his help, and he helped them all. I, Harrier from the Three Rapids, have seen him order the spirits to him and make them talk, interrogate them, and show them where wrong has been done! So he healed those who suffered undeservedly.

"But his enemy was never safe. However far he tried to flee, the curse of Shelk would reach him in the end. He would die a painful death, and the Guardian of the hyena would receive his carcass."

Harrier was silent for a while, gloating over the dreadful fate of Shelk's enemies. Whitespear looked up from his work and met Kite's eyes. She grinned and winked at him, then looked perfectly serious again.

Harrier drank.

"We lived in pride and joy under his outstretched arm. But the evil Powers leagued together and raged against him. They called on the Great River, and it fell over us and annihilated all that Shelk had created. Then he made his supreme sacrifice and threw his own body into the churning waters."

Whitespear got up. He had captured his picture. He handed it to Harrier, who held it up in the firelight. Whitespear had begun by painting a soot-black background that called to mind the dark wall of the forest and the night sky, and had covered it with shapes carved into the white bone. There was the anthill, red with ochre, the color of life, and crowned with two great shelk antlers, like wings unfolding. There were the slender, light birch stems, pointing skyward and conveying a sense of mystery and hidden meaning. On high shone the constellation of stars they knew as the Mammoth. Sitting at his work, Whitespear had seen it come out in the twilit northern sky and felt that he had found his own sign. Henceforward he would sign all his handiwork in that way.

Harrier was visibly moved. "You could become a shaman, my dear Whitespear," he said. "There is magic in this picture. I can feel that in my fingertips. It will have great power."

"It is yours, Harrier," said Whitespear.

The Shaman put his hand on his heart and bowed. "I shall keep it always. You have made me a great gift, my boy. With the necessary words, it will carry the power of Shelk."

He murmured a charm in a language unknown to Whitespear. But he could see that Kite knew it, for she listened raptly, and her lips moved in silent repetition of the words.

. . .

The moon, in its second quarter, was brilliant in the dark sky. Harrier resumed his story.

"We were the true disciples of Shelk. We searched for him, and after many days we found him. What we found was only his body, but we knew that his spirit was alive and that his powers would never fade. None of us knew what to do, but I, Harrier from the Three Rapids, was entrusted with the task of finding his living spirit in the darkness.

"You have drunk the shaman wine, Whitespear, so my daughter tells me: it gave you the power to render that picture. It gives pleasure as well as insight. But the sacred potion, the one that opens the road to the land of the spirits, is something else, and you have to spend winters and summers preparing for it. Drunk by the uninitiated, it leads to death. That potion I took, while the disciples uttered the secret words, and the ordinary world around me faded away. I roved widely in the land of the spirits, I wandered through many forests, I crossed many rivers. I was led astray by false stars, I was chilled by the snow and burned by the sun. Gnats and midges drank my blood, lions and bears raged at me—

but in the end I stood before his face. He saw me and he whispered three words, and that whisper was like a thunder-clap.

"I woke among the disciples. They had kept watch over me for a day and a night, and they received me back with wonder and joy: Boar from the Land of Flints, Eagle from the Hill, Whitebear from the shore of the Salt Sea. Together, we interpreted the meaning of Shelk's words.

"I remembered well what Shelk told me once, when he still walked on the earth. The ants, he said, build greater houses and fight greater wars than any other creatures: do not despise them. Theirs is the final power over mammoths and men, wolves and tigers. So he wished his body given to the ants, so that it might live forever. And it was done as he had wished. Here we found the greatest anthill in the world, and this is the resting-place of Shelk. From here, his power emanates. And so I became the Shaman of Horn Lake Village, which is close by."

Whitespear was deeply awed. He had heard many stories about Shelk, but he had never dreamed that he would see Shelk's grave. Soon the warmth of summer would call its inhabitants back to life. The spirit of that Master of masters would issue from it.

Harrier was talking still, his spirits rising with the shrink-ing of his wineskin. Whitespear was told that this place was a sanctuary to which Harrier would repair when he tired of Swidden Moor and especially of Otter, whom he found a difficult man to stand. This had happened once again last summer when Otter managed to incense Harrier more than usual just before leaving with his men for the Summer Meet. Harrier did not disclose the reason. Later on, however, Kite told Whitespear that the flare-up resulted from Otter's un-fortunate predilection for maladroit proverbs. While Otter mustered his men before leaving (he wanted them to look their best), Harrier was feasting on forest strawberries, a present from a mother whose child he had nursed back to

health. Otter's comment—"Yes, the calf knows how to find
the teat"—had left Harrier speechless with rage.

Since then, Harrier and Kite had lived in their camp near
Shelk's grave. They were often visited by journeying shamans and apprentices, who knew the place well, and had in
fact lived a pampered life, for their guests would bring them
all kinds of gifts and do most of the hunting. Still, Kite was
getting bored, and had decided to bring about a reconciliation.

It now seemed that she had succeeded. Harrier squeezed
the last drop from his wineskin, brandished it, and cried,
"Now I shall go back to Horn Lake Village. Already, the
first calls of the cranes are being heard, and the moon waxes
round. The Crane Feast will be held, and Swidden Moor
needs its Shaman. But you, Whitespear, must go your own
way to your island, and Kite will go with you. I have made
her ready: whatever I could do to help your father, she can
do too. And she will learn the arts of your Troll shamans,
whom you call healers, and bring them back to me."

Excited by these prospects, Harrier got up, and was surprised to find his legs very wobbly. He started to sing a song,
took a few floundering steps, then seemed to get his legs
entangled with each other, and fell with a crash. Whitespear
and Kite helped him into his hut, where he immediately fell
asleep, smiling like a happy child.

Whitespear wrapped his cloak around him and lay down
under the stars. After a while he felt Kite's hand in his own.
So they slept, hand in hand, and the spring night was silent
around them in the white light of the moon.

·   ·   ·

Nobody saw him enter the village.

He had no wish to reveal himself to Otter. He was going
to Veyde's Island, and Siskin would go with him as his
woman. Otter most certainly would not like the idea. Silent

and preoccupied, he had pondered these prospects during the journey with Kite and Harrier.

It would be a long march, and the cloudberries would be in bloom before they arrived at the island. Already the last mammoths had gone north. The cranes were flying, and the air reverberated with their calls from on high. Spring was blowing into the land with the cranes.

When they approached Swidden Moor, Whitespear stopped, wishing Harrier and Kite to precede him. Harrier took no notice; he walked on, his arms crossed over his chest, but Kite turned to Whitespear with a look of surprise. He signed to her to go on.

When they were out of sight, he crept on and finally climbed a tree from where he could look out over the village. He saw that the people had collected around the holy Sun Pillar, which stood on a hill near the beaver dam, and he realized that the spring feast had started, the celebration during which the cranes were welcomed and prayers were made to the Guardians for the speedy arrival of the shelk. Siskin would surely be there, beautifully ornamented and proud, and Otter would give one of his great speeches. Whitespear made a face. All this fuss about the Sun Pillar was strange to him. True, Tiger had erected a pillar like that on Veyde's Island, but it was left in peace, and was not annoyed with prayers and invocations.

He saw Otter and Harrier step into the circle, side by side. So they had met and become reconciled. Otter embraced the Shaman, who remained stiff and unresponsive, and the people burst into jubilant cheers. Otter enjoined silence and started to talk. He had a carrying voice, and fragments of his speech reached Whitespear's ears.

"Our beloved Shaman . . . greatest of shamans . . . For many moons, struggling with the Powers . . . Solitary like the wolverine on the moor . . . Solitary like the moon in the sky . . ."

At this point, Harrier began to fidget and Whitespear

could guess at his angry mumblings. To be likened to the moon rather than the Sun would hardly gratify his ambitious heart. Whitespear grinned. Clearly, Otter was in his best form.

". . . returned," the Chief went on, "like the mother wolf to her cubs . . . Lick their wounds . . . Remember: Watch the wood, await the stag!" (Which meant Do not wait, go to work!) ". . . He who wants meat in the morning has to hunt at night . . ."

Much later, Whitespear would look back at the Crane Feast and Otter's oratory with new understanding. They all lived surrounded by the Powers, dark and secret, some of them benevolent, some malignant: the world was full of them. Dimly, Whitespear realized that Otter with his proverbs, with the collected treasury of sayings that expressed his people's entire life and traditional wisdom, was trying to allay and appease the Unknown. Was he, Whitespear, perhaps doing the same thing when he brought his pictures into the world? Harrier sought security in his sorcery and his secret language; the Whites, in their rituals and courtesies; Siskin, in her treasures. All this came to him many, many years later, dimly, because he did not have words to express it.

He could not see Siskin in all that crowd. Never mind: he would wait for her in their house. Their reunion, and all that he had to tell her, now filled him to the exclusion of everything else.

He walked rapidly to the house. He did not meet anybody. In the distance he could hear Otter: ". . . Where horses are plentiful, the snow is patterned with tracks . . ."

There she stood, her hair streaming in the wind!

Her eyes were round with astonishment. She stretched her hands out to him, and in one hand there glowed a pearl.

"Oh!" Whitespear said in surprise. "So it was to *you* that Lamey gave the pearl?"

She swayed as if she had received a slap in the face. The

immensity of the shame and despair that engulfed her was something she had never experienced. She saw herself as the others would—debased, ridiculed. Her vision dimmed so that she could hardly see Whitespear's face, yet she thought she could see bitterness and scorn in it. In the next breath a savage fury welled up in her and burned away the shame. "Go away!" she screamed. "Go away! I never want to see you again! Go!"

She was crouching before him like a wild animal. Whitespear drew back in the face of her fury. He could understand nothing. "Go!" she said again, in a lower voice but with such vehemence that he obeyed her at once. He turned his back and went away blindly, without comprehension.

She remained standing, her hands clenched, till he was out of sight. Then the nausea came back, and she threw herself to the ground and vomited.

"When the horses are dead, the lion mourns . . ." droned Otter in the distance.

KITE

The journey from Swidden Moor to Veyde's Island, far away in the east, was to last almost a whole moon. When they set out, the magical and solemn dance of the cranes was just beginning on the marsh meadows across Horn Lake from the village: a spectacle full of augury and foreboding that was followed intently by the people, mimicked in their own dances during the Crane Feast, and interpreted by soothsayers.

They departed in the time of the full moon and trekked east across a land that was stirred by the coming of spring, through endless pine forests where the birdsong was almost deafening. The play of the capercaillies was still going on, and one of the cocks, mistaking Kite for a rival, came rushing at her in distracted fury. They killed and ate it.

Whitespear had left without Siskin, without his woman, so they were only two: Whitespear and Kite.

She asked him about Siskin, but Whitespear did not answer. He was downhearted and still unable to understand what had happened. Silently, he reviewed his life with Siskin and tried to make out where he had been at fault. He could find no answer. At the same time there was a curious feeling of relief mingled with his sadness—relief that a confused part of his life had come to an end. He would never see her again.

She had become a picture—no, many pictures, and they kept rising to his inner eye. Maybe she would remain with him like that for all his life. One day, perhaps, he would be able to bring forth those pictures for others to see. Not now —later. Maybe those pictures were what the Powers had intended when they tricked him, when they made a fool of him. He raged inwardly against their iniquity.

Kite did not repeat her question. She realized that something very untoward had happened and that Whitespear did not want to talk about it. She was burning with curiosity, but her shaman discipline kept her in check. She was by nature a very impulsive girl, and in the past her impetuosity had landed her in trouble many times. There were things that did not become a shaman. A shaman was expected to be solemn, reticent, and oracular and to maintain a reputation for powers beyond those of ordinary people. That was Harrier's teaching, repeated over and over, and only too often in indignant tones, with impatient gestures, when she had forgotten herself. Sometimes she had spoken out of turn. Once she had even broken into undignified tittering when she saw her father coach a novice in some ritual that happened to strike her as funny. Those memories smarted, and Kite would tell herself, sometimes several times a day, that she must remember to be dignified and behave in a truly shamanlike manner.

Not that Harrier himself invariably lived up to his teaching —a shaman should not fly into rages. But an old man like him could get away with it, while a young shamaness like herself would only look silly.

So instead Kite asked Whitespear about Veyde's Island, about the Whites and their way of life, about the hunting of the seal and the bison, about fishing, about the birds the Whites held sacred (especially the swan and the long-tailed duck), about Tiger and Veyde and Helleborine. Whitespear found that talking of such things helped him forget his own troubles, and so Kite came to know the whole story of his life, except for the part that concerned Siskin. She listened with close attention, for her shaman upbringing had made her a good learner, and she stored it all in her memory as well as she could. Knowledge, Harrier had taught her, was the road to power; and her greatest wish was to become a famous shaman.

She could see herself many summers hence, revered and beloved as the foremost interpreter of Shelk's decisions and the foremost wielder of his power. Maybe sometimes she would make a journey, for instance, to cure somebody who was very ill, or to decide a difficult dispute, or perhaps to give Shelk's benediction to the newborn child of a chief. Mostly, though, she would reside in her chosen village, surrounded by a devoted clan, at the side of a handsome and popular chief (casting a glance at Whitespear, Kite decided that he would be a very suitable chief). From distant lands, messengers would come to her for counsel, and young shamans-to-be would seek her out, eager to learn from the great shamaness, famed for her wisdom. All over the land her name would be known, almost like that of Shelk. Thus Kite dreamed, and she smiled without being aware of it.

But although Kite thought of herself as dignified and aloof, she remained in fact a merry and talkative girl, always ready for a laugh or a prank. Sometimes she would affect an enigmatic look, stare at something far away, and try to listen for the spirits, in case they had something to tell her. This time, however, it was Whitespear who asked:

"Kite, you have heard my story, but I know nothing about you. Where do you hail from yourself?"

Kite, who had just found that you were apt to stumble over a root if you stared into the distance, had a momentary relapse into reticence and said, "But you know that, Whitespear. I am the daughter of Harrier, greatest of shamans."

A glance at Whitespear made her relent. After all, he spoke the Language, and Harrier himself had said that he had the makings of a shaman. Besides, she was not going to reveal any secrets.

"Well, if you really want to know, I was born in Horn Lake Village. My father was Harrier from the Three Rapids, and my mother was Squirrel daughter of Stoat."

Her eyes were shining now. "Did you know that Shelk's own mother too was called Squirrel—isn't that wonderful? Why, it must be an omen," she cried eagerly, and in the next breath regretted her words. She had talked out of turn again! To cover her confusion, she went on rapidly, "But they don't live together any more. He threw her out!"

Worse and worse! She felt her cheeks burning. Memories of that old scandal, when she was about two hands old, assailed her: violent scenes, the villagers shouting and laughing. She looked covertly at Whitespear, half expecting a supercilious smile. But he just looked astonished.

"Why did he do that?" asked Whitespear. He tried to picture a White man throwing out his woman. The idea was so weird that he felt his head swimming. Of course, a White woman could repudiate her man, and then he would have to go. On the other hand, if the man tired of his woman, the custom was for him to leave the village altogether and go somewhere else.

Kite felt encouraged, and decided to be frank. "She deceived him. He used to spend a lot of time in his camp by Shelk's grave. Sometimes I went with him, sometimes I stayed in the village with my mother. She'd always wanted a son, but I was just a girl, and Harrier never gave her another child. There was a man in the village who used to come to her. He was called Badger. I didn't like him, but Mother did, and he gave her a son. My father was enraged."

Her artless story left Whitespear gaping. If a White woman wanted a child and her man was unable to give her one, then his duty was to enlist help. He himself, Whitespear, had been such a child, with Tiger as Baywillow's substitute. He told Kite, and she smiled gratefully.

"Then they went away—Badger, my mother, and their child. They are living at Falcon Hill now. And my father was very lenient. He didn't put a curse on them, though he could have done so. He's much kinder than people think. He almost never curses anybody."

"Hmm," said Whitespear, scratching his nose. "I thought I heard him call Otter a name or two. A woodlouse, or something."

"Yes, of course, but that isn't real cursing. If a shaman puts a real curse on you, you're not going to live for long. You'll waste away, and the Guardian of the hyena will get you. There is no evading the revenge of Shelk."

Whitespear shuddered. Better be wary of shamans, he thought.

"But my father didn't do that," Kite said reassuringly. "A good shaman is forbearing and saves his curses. That's what he says."

She checked herself. Maybe I'm talking too much again, she thought. Still, we may yet make a shaman out of Whitespear too. And she felt suddenly happy, as if a great burden had been taken off her shoulders.

That night they stopped by a small stream, and Whitespear set some traps for woodfowl and hares.

· · ·

They went on at a leisurely pace, avoiding the low-lying ground, which was soggy with meltwater. Along the eskers

the walking was firm and the plant-cover sparse in the shade
of the stately pines. The wood anemones were coming into
flower like new-fallen snow. They crossed several small rivers teeming with fish, and usually did so astride a log. It was
a handy way but had one drawback: the ice-cold water left
their legs numb, and when they arrived at the opposite bank,
they would run and dance, jump and spin around, laughing
and yelling, until they felt warm again.

Then they came to the Big River, which they would have
to cross. Whitespear knew that it started from Caribou Lake
far to the northwest, Shelk's domain of old. Farther down
its course it widened into Big Lake, where he had been a
moon ago to look for Harrier and had found the village
deserted. This time, however, they came to the river far
downstream from Big Lake, in a place where it formed a
series of rapids. They decided to make the crossing well
above the rapids, where the river was broader but the current
quite gentle. In the middle of the river was an island where
they could stop to rest.

In the summer, crossing a large river was easy enough. A
raft of sorts could be made out of interlaced pine-boughs to
carry gear. Then one had only to swim across, pushing the
raft. But it was spring now, and the water much too cold for
swimming, so Whitespear and Kite had to make a real raft,
big enough to carry them both. They found a couple of fallen
trees that were dry but not yet rotten, and labored for a
whole day hacking them into logs, which were then tied
together with thongs.

The crossing went without a hitch, and they decided to
stay for a couple of days to fish. The salmon were coming
up the river in tremendous numbers, forcing themselves up
the cataracts in flashing leaps. Whitespear made two fishing-
spears, using fishbones as barbs. Then they went to work.
They did so well that they could gorge themselves on fresh
salmon, and they smoked as many as they would be able to
carry. Dried, the fish would be a lighter load, but that was

not to be thought of here, where so many carnivores flocked to the rapids. The smell of drying fish would certainly attract bears and wolverines to their camp, even though they placed it well away from the rapids, and if they put the fish up in the trees, ravens and eagles would get at them.

Whitespear and Kite now felt like old friends. The companionship of the journey, their long talks about personal matters, and the sheer fun of dancing and laughing together had drawn them closer. So it came about that one evening, as they were resting after the day's work, Whitespear started to talk about that most difficult subject: Siskin.

Kite listened intently. Before long, she understood perfectly the reason for Siskin's behavior, which was so puzzling to Whitespear, and for a moment she felt pity for the ill-starred daughter of the Swidden Moor Chief. On an impulse, she cried out, "But don't you see—"

She stopped. She now knew that Siskin had rejected him for fear of being humiliated. After having heard Whitespear's account of the people on Veyde's Island, though, she knew that he would have judged the matter quite differently, not like the ordinary Black man, not like her father Harrier in the same situation. He would not condemn Siskin. Maybe he would regard what she had done as quite natural and reasonable.

Would he go back to Siskin, if she revealed this to him? She looked thoughtfully at Whitespear. She herself did not much care for the Chief's proud daughter, who looked down her nose at everybody else. No: he was really too good for her. She would only make him unhappy again. That, she felt, was a truly shamanlike decision for the best.

Whitespear looked at her expectantly. But she did not have a chance to say anything, for at that very moment there was a loud crashing in the alders. Something broke forth, threw itself on the ground at their feet, and screamed:

"Mercy! Mercy for the evildoer! Mercy for the cursed people of Caribou Lake! Mercy for the wretched!"

The thing that lay writhing, in a paroxysm of weeping, was the wreck of a White man, and he had called out to them in the language of the Whites.

. . .

The White man was dreadfully emaciated, a skeleton meagerly draped in sinews and skin, and his mighty rib-cage rose like a vault over his shrunken midriff. Naked and shivering, he was utterly out of his wits and was only able to weep and pray for mercy.

Kite took charge at once. She ripped a piece of skin off the roof of the little hut that Whitespear had built for them. She ran down to the river and returned with the skin full of water. This she promptly emptied over the face of the prostrate man.

"Get me a bigger skin, Whitespear," she ordered.

When he returned with what was left of the hut-cover, he found Kite eyeing the man curiously. He was still lying on his back, spluttering and moaning, but the shock of the cold water had pulled him out of his hysterics.

"Well," Kite said to herself, with some disappointment, "it's not all that big, I think."

"What isn't?" asked Whitespear. Kite, suddenly embarrassed, flushed darkly and did not answer. She covered the man up with the skin and said, "Let's move him closer to the fire. He's shivering with cold."

When they had carried the man to the fire, Whitespear repeated his question. "Well, it's the first time I've ever seen a Troll," said Kite defensively. "They look very odd, don't they? And the women used to tell all sorts of stories about them, and they always said that their—ah—well, that it was ve-e-ery big, much bigger than in a man, and stone hard—"

"Oh, their cock!" said Whitespear, enlightened.

"As big as a pine-branch, they said. And *very* rough. Like bark."

Whitespear was grinning broadly. "It's no different from ours."

"Well, it's—ah—white. Or pink, rather."

"They are Whites, you know. And they are not really Trolls. They are people, just like us."

"They look so odd, don't they? That great chest, and those eyebrows. They look . . . dangerous."

"Well, they're not. They're very mild, and very good-mannered. Can you save him, Kite?"

"I'll try. Tell me—do they always go around naked like that?"

"No, only when it's warm."

"The women too?"

"Yes."

Kite shook her head in wonder. "What do they look like? The girls, I mean."

"Much the same as he does. Only, they're girls."

"Are they pretty?"

Whitespear scratched his head. "Not as pretty as you, Kite." And for the first time he realized that she was indeed very pretty, though quite different from Siskin.

"They sound very odd," Kite sighed. "Still, my father told me to learn their arts. I will do my best for this man."

She opened her medicine bag and pulled out a small bison-calf horn with a wooden stopper. When she took out the stopper, he could smell the honey inside. She dipped her forefinger into it, then held it up in the air and recited a charm in a strange language. The man was looking at her fearfully, but when Kite forced her finger between his lips he closed his eyes and sucked it. She nodded, and repeated the procedure several times.

"Shelk means him to live," said Kite. "He's keeping the food down."

"What were the words you said just then?" asked White-spear.

"The High Language." She reflected for a moment. "I can

tell you this, because my father says that you may become a shaman. They say it was spoken in the old days. Shelk learned it from an old man when he collected all the wisdom of the living world. It is very potent, and almost never fails."

"Can I help?"

"Yes, you can collect a bagful of last year's lingonberries. And some wood sorrel. They are just coming into flower."

She worked indefatigably with the exhausted man. Whitespear was deeply impressed. He had seen Helleborine the healer in action but Kite was something very different. She read many spells in the strange High Language. She fed the man berries, honey, and wood sorrel, but made no attempt to give him fish, of which they had plenty; he was not ready for that yet, she said. She donned a lynx-skin hat, evidently her badge of office, and danced in a circle around the man, waving two sticks and repeating powerful incantations. Sometimes she spoke soothing words in the White language, and this seemed to reassure the man, who looked at her with great wonder but remained mute. At last he fell asleep, and Kite sat down exhausted.

"We'll have to stay here for a few days, until he regains his strength," she said. "I think he is under Shelk's protection and we are meant to help him. But what shall we do with him?"

"We can't leave him. He has lost everything, even his clothes. He wouldn't go unclothed at this time of the year. We'd better take him with us to Veyde's Island."

Kite nodded and took another look at her patient. "He's sleeping soundly now. He'll be better tomorrow. Whitespear, I don't think those women knew anything at all about Trolls. They said the Troll oxen would rape a Black woman, and their strength and prowess was such that she'd become their slave. And that the Troll bitches have teeth in their vaginas, and much more like that."

Whitespear laughed. "You'll see for yourself, when we come to the island."

They stayed by the rapids, and as a result of Kite's skillful nursing, the wretched man began to recover and eventually was able to take solid food. Yet he remained confused and incoherent. He only managed to stutter a few words, and he was forever making the sign of submission and propitiation, clapping his hands over his eyes.

At last he was able to stand up, and they took him along, supported between them.

He often repeated his plea for mercy, but they were unable to find out what crime he had committed. He seemed convinced that they knew all about his sin, and perhaps hoped that they had the power to release him from it. Whitespear knew that many of the Whites regarded the Blacks as higher beings, even godlike, and he tried to assure the man that he was forgiven, but to no avail. Finally, one evening Kite dressed up in full shaman finery, made a long oration in the Black language, and read a powerful spell. Then the man realized that he had nothing more to fear and said that he was now ready to die in peace.

"You are not going to die," said Kite. "You are coming with us to Veyde's Island."

"I hear and obey, Miss Kite," said the man humbly.

He was mending fast, and soon was able to walk without support. Gradually, they drew out his story. His name, they learned, was Heather, and he hailed from Caribou Lake; and as far as he knew, he was the sole survivor of his tribe. All the others had been destroyed by the Powers because of the enormity of their sins. He had only expected that he would die, too, and would certainly not go to the Land of Birds after death.

Heather did not tell his story coherently, however. Rambling, sometimes raving, he jumped from one thing to another, always returning to the burden of his sins, a burden that he now had to shoulder alone because there were no others living. Yet the outline of his narrative was coming through. Suddenly, the truth dawned upon Whitespear. He was being told why he had found the Big Lake village abandoned.

What he did not realize at that time, but was to find out later, was that Avens was crossing his tracks once more, moving unseen and unknown as before, looming and ever larger, more masterful, more ominous.

.   .   .

Whitespear told Oriole:

"Heather's story began with the day when the summer turned and the last ospreys left Caribou Lake. The Land of the Osprey, that was what they called the country around there, and the osprey was their sacred bird. On that day their leader died. She was called Miss Wintergreen, and she died between one breath and the next, stricken by the Powers, falling to the ground before their eyes. She died long before her time, at the very peak of her strength and wisdom. She had been a healer as well as a leader, and her people had loved her dearly.

"They laid her in her grave near the Great River, and her oldest son made the oration. She had three sons, all of them children of the Gods—by which he meant that they were Brown, the sons of a Black father and a White mother. In her young days, Miss Wintergreen had had a Black man, one of Shelk's warriors. That was long ago, and Heather was too young to remember him. When he was gone, Miss Wintergreen had devoted all her life to the tribe of which she became a leader. They had lived in happiness all those summers and winters, as long as Heather could remember.

"Every grown woman and man put the thing they prized most highly in their leader's grave, for her to keep in the Land of the Birds, but into her right hand they put the Treasure of treasures, the holy Smokestone. Heather said it made its owner invincible and would scare off all enemies, and that it put a spell over the game so that hunting was easy. They wanted Miss Wintergreen to have it for her afterlife. I don't know what the Smokestone was. Heather seemed to think we knew all about it, being Gods ourselves."

Oriole smiled. "I think I know what it was. And I think I know something about Miss Wintergreen's three Brown sons, too. But tell me more, please, Whitespear."

"Now that she was gone, and the Smokestone too, their luck broke. There was no one who felt equal to the leadership. They had a bad autumn, waiting in vain for the caribou to come up from the North. They prayed for a token from the Guardians, yet when the sign came nobody grasped its meaning. Suddenly their land was invaded by a horde of waxwings. They alighted in the rowans and feasted on the berries, which were plentiful that autumn. Soon all the birds started to behave as if unhinged. They would fly backwards and sideways as often as straight ahead, said Heather, and they would bump into trees and people and fall to the ground, helpless. Never before had Heather seen such a spectacle. Much later, some of the old people remembered that the same thing had happened many winters ago, at the time Shelk came to Caribou Lake and made the Whites his slaves.

"At last they were saved. The Guardian of the mammoth stepped down to the earth, appeared at Caribou Lake, and told them what to do."

"The Guardian of the mammoth!" exclaimed Oriole incredulously.

"Yes, that's what we said too, Kite and I. I saw his cloud-shape when a young boy, and Tiger saw him in a vision, but we had never heard of him walking the earth. Heather told us that the Guardian appeared before them in the guise of a woman and that she came together with a great single-tusked mammoth! She was covered with mammoth hair so he couldn't see her face, but from the way she spoke and moved he knew she was a woman, and no ordinary woman, more like a Goddess, taller than the White women. For all that, Heather came to doubt in the end that she was what she pretended to be, and to suspect that she was that trickster, the Guardian of the hyena.

"I know now who she was. She was Avens; she herself told me so. I believe that the thing she did at that time, in the guise of the mammoth's Guardian, made her more desperate and resolved than ever. And it was gruesome.

"When Heather told us of the single-tusked mammoth, I said that I had seen him too and that he was indeed the greatest mammoth bull in the world, with only the left tusk remaining, and it was immense. Heather said no, it was the right tusk! I thought he was still befuddled: the poor man had been so confused. But he told his story several times and insisted that it was the right tusk—he had seen it with his own eyes. I didn't know what to think. Maybe it was sorcery. To the Guardians all things are possible.

"*Now* I know. That came much later, though.

"Their luck changed. The Guardian made her home in a hut on top of a hill overlooking Caribou Lake and close to the great waterfall. Heather knew that it had been Shelk's eyrie in the old times, but since then nobody had dared go there. Now it became the Guardian's house, and the sons of Miss Wintergreen, the Brown ones, were the only people admitted there.

"When the tribe went out hunting, the Guardian stepped down from her hill and gave them a magic potion, which gave them power over the game, and so the hunting was good. It was a wondrous drink. With it in their blood, they felt strength and recklessness in their limbs. They killed the mammoth and the bison, the caribou and the bear, and suffered no more privations. When they had killed an animal they would sacrifice the best part to the Guardian, and Miss Wintergreen's sons told them that she received it with pleasure.

"Soon the magic potion had such power over them that they wished to serve the Guardian forever, just to enjoy it and the comfort that it gave. It made you feel immensely powerful, and it didn't matter that you were weak and tired afterwards, for by then there would be lots of meat to eat. Yet in the end it brought them to ruin.

"When the autumn was at its darkest they went hunting once more, all but one old woman, Miss Sorrel by name, who stayed with the children. This time the Guardian herself came along to guide them. It was a long journey, and they killed some game as they moved south. Then came the last dark night, and the Guardian gave them her magic potion and commanded them to fight. They were to destroy a nest of devils and evil spirits and their brood, who had offended the Guardians and corrupted the land. In reality, it was the Big Lake Village, which I had found empty in my quest for Harrier. The devils, she told them, were responsible for all their privations that autumn. And such was the strength of the potion that she now gave them, and so compelling her words, that they were seized with a furious rage and fell upon that devils' village in the dark of the night and killed everybody in it—women, men, and children.

"That morning the snow fell and the land became white, and they woke to their senses and to unquenchable terror in that white country. So potent had the magic been that less than half of their number rose to life. They saw their dead friends and wailed for despair. But even worse was the sight of all those whom they had killed in their madness, for they had the mark of innocence on their brows.

"For the sorrow that now seized them there was no consolation. They had committed the worst offense in the world. The Guardian was gone, she who had led them to perdition, and so were Miss Wintergreen's sons. All that remained for them was to dig a grave for all those who had died that night, and to await their own doom.

"They kept together, though they could hardly stand the sight of each other, for they saw their own guilt mirrored in the faces of their friends. They managed to get back to Caribou Lake, and there the final tragedy occurred. They went out hunting, but one of the men, who was too weak to go, stayed behind with Miss Sorrel and the children. While they were away he crept up to the Guardian's house and found the last skin of the magic drink. After drinking it, he was possessed with the Guardian of the hyena. He killed all the children, and finally threw himself into a deep pothole beneath Dry Falls, a place where Caribou Lake debouched in the old time. The woman was the only survivor, and after telling them the story she threw herself down after the man.

"There was little more to tell. They left Caribou Lake and wandered hither and thither, and one after the other died, for they had lost the will to live. Heather could not remember much about his dismal wanderings, or how he had managed to keep alive, or why he had lost all his belongings.

"Now Kite had given him back his life. He wanted to be her servant and slave forever. When he had unburdened himself, he became very happy. One day he got himself a lump of resin and started to chew it, and from that day he was always seen chomping away cheerfully on that everlasting morsel. That, he told us, was a sure sign that he would live; one of his misfortunes had been to lose the taste for resin, but now all was well."

THE · MAN · WHO · CALLED HIMSELF · GREYSEAL

The tansy was coming into bloom and the bilberries turning purple when the man who had been called Lamey returned to Swidden Moor. He still had a crooked back and a short leg, but there was a great change in him. Once shy and retiring, he now had the carriage of a conqueror and a flood of words.

The treasure he brought to Siskin surpassed anything else she had seen. It was a great rock crystal the size of her own hand, transparent, yet filled with smoke that seemed to drift and change when she turned the thing over. It made her think of the woodsmoke that must have covered Swidden Moor so many years ago when the forest burned. Maybe some of that great pall of smoke had found its way into the stone.

"It is for the loveliest," he said. "It is for you, Siskin, and you will go with me to the Salt Sea, where I shall be Greyseal, the Chief of Oyster Village. For the man they called Lamey is no more. I am Greyseal now."

Then, looking at her, he realized what had happened, and a proud smile appeared on his face.

"You . . . you are carrying my child!"

Siskin was silent. She was staring at the magical stone.

"Ah!" said the man who called himself Greyseal. "I shall have a son! My firstborn will be called Horned Owl after my father, and he will be Chief after me."

Siskin looked straight at him for the first time, and there was a dangerous glint in her eye.

"My child already has a name," she said in her clear voice.

"Oh! and what is it?" asked the man, momentarily shaken out of his euphoria.

"My child's name is Oriole," said Siskin, with finality in her voice.

"Oriole . . . Oriole," repeated the man uncomfortably. "Yes . . . yes, it's a good name. But you will come with me, won't you?" he went on, with a whine in his voice.

She looked long and hard at him, until he lowered his gaze. "Yes, I will come with you."

The man perked up immediately. "Yes, I thought you would," he said breezily. "And I'll do the right thing. I'll give your father a ransom he won't even have dreamed of. I have other things in my pack." He patted his bulky bag. "Let's go to him right away."

"No need," said Siskin. "I will come with you now."

"But . . . but he'll be my enemy. He'll pursue us."

"He is out hunting and won't be back for days. He won't know where we are going. I wish it that way."

"In that case . . . It's robbing him . . . Yes, we'll do as you say . . ."

Siskin was not listening. She had taken out the pearl, which she wore concealed in her dress, and now weighed it in one hand against the rock crystal in the other. This one

was a tear of happiness; that one, an omen of fire and destruction. There was her fate: joy in one hand, vicissitude in
the other. The certainty of pleasure, the certainty of pain.
Yes, she had come to know pain very well this summer.
Never had she known such loneliness. She knew that the
people whispered behind her back, she knew that they
smiled with malicious joy. She despised them all. She despised her father, too, with his pompous, long-winded
ways. Life at Swidden Moor had become unbearable to her:
anything would be better, even a life with this odd, misshapen man. At least he was devoted to her and she would
be able to bend him to her will.

She held the crystal to her eyes. There was her future,
veiled in smoke. With a sigh she put the treasures away. This
was a farewell to her old life.

The man was fondling her belly. "My child . . . Oriole,"
he said hoarsely, for the touch of her flesh aroused a blinding
passion in him. "My woman, the only woman in my life.
I'll give you everything. I'll do everything for you. Siskin, I
want you now!"

Their eyes met. He could read nothing in hers, and he
looked away. His hands shivered, still stroking her body. He
was shaking all over.

"Come into the house," said Siskin.

"I will not dance on top of my child," said the man, trying
to sound jocular, but his voice was shaky. Siskin obediently
turned her back and crouched down. Free from her intimi-
dating gaze, he entered her and within a single breath exploded into a premature orgasm that was oddly pallid and
different from what he had dreamed about. Siskin rose with
sperm trickling down her haunches, smiled at him, and said,
"You're a fast worker, Greyseal. You must learn to give me
more time."

"Yes," said the man humbly.

She did not pursue her advantage. She had him and she

knew it. "There will be many other times," she said kindly. "Let us go!"

. . .

He talked incessantly during their long westward journey, even though he panted under the heavy burden of his pack, which now contained not only all his gear and provisions but also Siskin's treasures. In his talk he jumped from one thing to another, but he always came back to the day when he found the rock crystal and took over from his brother Greyseal. She did not really listen, but fragments of his story were to remain with her.

"And do you know where I found it? No? It was a cache! A great Troll chief was buried there, with all his Troll treasure! And I found it! They wouldn't believe me, my brother and that youngster Weasel—no, they laughed, my brother laughed at me and young Weasel laughed with him. Yet there it was plain to be seen, a mound with a cairn on top! *I* knew what it was."

He gave her bottom a jolly slap, and she smiled mechanically.

"Would they had stayed with me! But no, 'We'll go to the river,' said my brother, 'we'll get some fish: the salmon are running.' And away they went, leaving me at the mound.

"I rolled away the stones. Oh yes, I'm stronger than you think! And there was a spear among the stones, so I knew I was right. A Troll spear!

"The Troll chief was there too, under the stones—he lay grinning at me with all his great teeth. But he dared not rise, and I took his treasure. I took it all! That smokestone was clenched in his hand, but he couldn't keep it. I was stronger than he, and I took it. So much the poorer he, so much the richer I. And now I'm rich beyond measure, for I have you —you and my child! Oriole," he said, as if trying it out,

"Oriole . . . Yes, a good name. Chief Oriole! Sounds fine, doesn't it? Yes, he will succeed Chief Greyseal." And he went on talking about Oyster Village on the Salt Sea, and what people would say when he came back, all changed, rich, with a beautiful woman and a child to come, he whom they had known as Lamey!

"But I am Greyseal now! And Chief Diver, who succeeded my father, is old and doddery, and has no son. But we have a good shaman, Whitebear by name—he will help you when Oriole's time comes. My son! My woman! I'm a man now, as I never was. I am Greyseal!"

He was puffing heavily under his burden. "Time to rest," he said and put it down. "We'll have to hunt soon. There isn't much left to eat. Pick some berries for me, my woman," he ordered and lay down.

When she returned with the bilberries, he was ready to take up his tale.

"I sang and danced around that Troll chief, and he just lay there, grinning as happy as ever. But I covered him up again. There is no danger—the cairn is back on top of him, so he can't get out. He sleeps in peace. Why, he didn't need the treasure any more, you could see that. But I needed it! And it gave me my life! So, maybe he really wanted me to have it. Because, just see what happened next!

"I was tracking my brother down to the river, and then I heard a terrible commotion, screams and curses, and when I came to the riverbank there were three terrible men there, and two men lying on the ground with spears sticking out of them, and those two were my brother and young Weasel, and they would laugh no more. Those men saw me, and they came at me with spear and axe! But I held the smoke-stone in my hand, for I had intended to show it to my brother and let him know what he missed when he left that cairn unexplored. I was holding it out, and those three men saw it and stopped. They looked terrible to me, brown-skinned, with smoldering eyes under heavy brows—yes, not ordinary people at all! Half Trolls, I think they were.

"They had meant to kill me as they had killed my brother and young Weasel. But when they saw me with that shining stone, they were frightened. That stone has magic: it made me twice the size of a man! And they were frightened. They saw it and they ran away. They ran away, do you see? I just scared them away!

"Yes, I'm a real man now. I have a woman, I have a child, and I drove away the evildoers who killed my brother.

"There was breath in him still, and before he died he knew that I had the treasure. He had seen all that happened, and he smiled at me. 'You are Greyseal now,' he said. He died, and I buried him and Weasel on the bank of the Great River."

"How wonderful," said Siskin, stifling a yawn. She was feeling dispirited after the day's long trek and the berry picking. She wished that the man would procure some real food for them. But she held her peace. He would be really hungry soon, and know what was expected of him.

· · ·

Hunger overtook them slowly but inexorably. The man was not a good hunter, being mainly experienced as a game beater. They fed on berries until Siskin hated the sight and taste of them. They still toiled westward, slowly and painfully. Siskin did not complain. She had gone into her new life with open eyes, and her pride held her firm. Sometimes she would take out the rock crystal and look at it with a sardonic smile. This was part of the future that she had seen in it.

It was the horse that saved them in the end. They had sighted horses several times, but their speed was beyond the man who called himself Greyseal. This horse, however, was in such a wretched condition that it seemed a sheer miracle a hyena had not got it long ago. It was a stallion with a broken jaw, the result of a spirited kick by a mare who was by no means ready for its enthusiastic overtures, and the man killed it easily enough.

The cause of the injury was evident, and it gave the man a great laugh. "Ah, there, you see! Mark it, Siskin, that's how you treat the man you don't want." He was busy cutting up the carcass, which was very lean but still held enough meat to last them a long way. "We'll stay here for a while and eat our fill, and then we'll smoke the meat and pull it with us on runners. Yes, it'll last us to Oyster Village. The magic of the smokestone is working, don't you see? Why, by rights the wolves and hyenas would have had that horse long ago. The stone kept them away, just as it drove away those terrible men."

Gleefully, he slapped her bottom. *Maybe he is right,* thought Siskin. *That stone is giving him luck. Luck,* she thought desperately. *Luck is what I need. I've never had any, for all that I'm a chief's daughter. If the stone helps him, it will help me too. Maybe he really will become a chief.*

Yes, if every other man in that village is a cripple. She smiled in spite of herself. She was entering a new life indeed.

From that day, their luck changed for the better. They were now coming to rivers that wound their way to the west, to the Salt Sea, and the fishing was good. It did not matter that the weather turned foul for a few days, with torrents of rain and a howling southwestern gale. They were now well fed and spent most of the time in a shelter, where the man was making up for a lifetime of lost sexual opportunities. His repeated, laughing references to the luckless stallion would probably have driven her crazy if she had listened to him, but she took no notice of his unceasing talk.

More and more she withdrew into herself, and lost track of the days while they trudged on. The rain had ceased, but the weather was still cloudy and windy, and cold for the season. It only served to invigorate her: her strength was returning. Often she would finger the smokestone. Yes, it was giving her luck.

Then one day summer was back with sunny skies, and the man told her, "We are close to the sea now." They climbed the spur of a hill, and there, standing on the crest, she saw the sea for the first time in her life. She could hardly believe it was real, that distant, endless expanse of blue water. The man had put down his pack and was jumping and shouting for joy.

"There! Do you see it?" he cried, pointing. "I know this place. We're north of the village. We'll just go down to the coast, and then south for two days! We're almost there! Come, Siskin!" He gripped his pack and started to run downhill, still shouting.

And then, too late, he realized that he was running down a scree. Siskin screamed. All of the sloping ground around him broke loose and started to move. In a torrent of rolling rocks he ran on, his steps becoming impossibly long. He tried to stop, but everything was in raging motion, and he fell and vanished in an avalanche of stones.

She found him at the foot of the hill, half buried by the rocks but miraculously still alive. That battered, misshapen body seemed to hold an indomitable will to live. She dug him out and did what she could for him.

With many bones broken and much loss of blood, he was unable to move at first, though in a few days some of his strength came back. Then fever set in, and he raved helplessly for days. Shortly before the end he regained consciousness, his head cradled in her lap. His cheek was pressed to her belly.

"There will be no Chief Greyseal," he whispered. "But I can feel my son kicking within you. He will be big and strong. He will do all the things I never did. Oriole will be the Chief of Oyster Village in days to come."

She buried him, and for the second time in her life wept

bitterly for somebody else than herself. It had not happened since her mother's death.

She went on alone, and her sadness gradually gave way to a new emotion: she was feeling cleansed and strong. She held up the smokestone to her eyes. The man had given it to her, and he had lost his luck. Now the lucky stone was hers, and she would never give it up. Assured and poised, she walked towards Oyster Village. There was her future, and Oriole's.

BAYWILLOW

Strongest of all heavenly lights, the Morning Star
blazed over the forest edge, across the channel from
Veyde's Island. Already the spirits of morning had kindled a
red glow above the treetops. It would grow and light up
and, in the end, engulf that luminous point in the sky.

Tiger, standing on top of the knoll at Lookout Point,
strained his eyes to see through the dusk. The star was a lure
for his gaze and his thoughts. It was said now in the land
that this star was Shelk the Healer, rising at dawn to herald
his father the Sun. It was Shelk the Benign, and to see him
was the omen of good things to come. Such were the words
of Helleborine son of Silverbirch.

Beware of the other one, the Evening Star, trailing behind
the westering Sun and pulling the cloak of night after him!
That was Shelk the Destroyer, and his light was evil. Those

were the evenings of unrest and vigilance, evenings when you shielded your eyes from the fell rays.

Never the two were seen on the same day. The goodly star had his time, the ill star his. Now, and for many days past, was the time of the Morning Star, and Tiger was awaiting the return of his son.

There was a cold nip in the air, and Tiger gave a shiver. Frost silvered the tender grass in the cracks of the rock on which he was standing. Here, in the seaward skerries, the winter tarried long. Inland, the birches already sported small green leaves, but here alder and rowan were still naked.

It was all much simpler in the old days, he thought. You did not have all these worries. To be sure, the Powers might have struck him in the old days too, but they did so fairly, face to face. You could defend yourself! That he had done, he and his friends. He had seen Baywillow break the head of Shelk the Destroyer; he had seen Shelk the Healer flung to his death by the giant spirit of Caribou Lake. That was many winters ago, and the Powers had been on his side. Yet here was Shelk again, immortal, watchful, whispering, "I have never forgotten you."

So much to be done. To find out what the Powers intended. To put one's case to them, speak to them, appease them. They could stab you in the back by doing violence to your loved ones. There was no one more dear to him than that son he had been waiting for, day after day, ever since the Morning Star rose for the first time.

Suddenly he gave a low exclamation and shaded his eyes with his hand. Then he ran down to the shore, pushed out the raft, and poled it into deep water. The sky was lighting up while he paddled his clumsy craft across the channel, and a pipit started to try its voice. Tiger stepped ashore, pulled his raft up on the beach, and, stepping silently, ascended the knoll.

Smiling, he looked down at the sleepers. They were defenseless, deep in slumber: his son and the two others.

Whitespear slept with his face to the ground. Tiger studied him, and his heart was singing. The boy looked well, yes, grand, and by the Black Hill, his beard was growing!

Beside him a girl was curled up, her cheek resting on her arm. So Whitespear had found a woman—so small and tender, almost a child! No, her body was that of a grown woman. Then all had turned out for the best. The Powers were with him still.

Who could that White man be? He looked badly knocked about. Thin and worn, he lay on his back, snoring with open mouth. He must have had a rough time. Well, they would fatten him up on Veyde's Island. Tiger's love for his son spread like a wing over the boy's companions.

A chaffinch gave a penetrating trill, and the girl woke up. She sat up and met Tiger's smile. The resemblance between him and Whitespear was so strong that she knew right away who he was. "You are Tiger," she said, pushing back her hair. The movement revealed the red mark on her forehead.

"A shaman!" exclaimed Tiger. "And so young!"

Before she had time to answer, Whitespear rolled over and jumped up. "Tiger!" he cried, smiling.

Tiger embraced him. "Welcome back, *my son,*" he said with sudden gravity. As the meaning of the words dawned on Whitespear, his face turned grey.

"Then I was too late. I have been at fault."

"No. Nobody is to blame."

"Yes! We could have helped. *She* could have. Her art comes from Shelk the Healer. Only I did not find her until the end of the winter. I should have tried harder. I am to blame."

"No. It was his own choice."

.   .   .

It had happened three moons ago, Tiger told them; well he remembered the day. It was clear and cold, with dazzling snow—yes, the snow was so deep you sank in it to your knees. The sea was frozen as far as your eye could reach.

"The signs had been bad for a long time," he said. "The Powers were against us, and we were having poor luck. For several days, there had been a marauding wolf pack in the islands. They took hares and fowls from our traps. We did our best to get at them, but the rogues were too clever for us. Once, and once only, I caught sight of them: they were trekking in line across the ice. They moved along comfortably, their tails hanging, except the Chief himself. Right in the middle he was, the Chief of the wolves, his tail proudly in the air! Oh, he was a haughty one! He was lording it, with his people all around. He had outwitted us, time and again. He made me think of Shelk's right-hand man, Viper, whom we all hated in the old times. Viper met his fate in the end, but the wolf Chief got away. I'd have put a javelin into him, but he was out of range. I saw them walk up on the shore and vanish in the woods, all that long line of greylegs. One single trap they'd missed, and it held a hare, but Mullein came too late—a fox swiped the hare and made away with it right under her nose!

"On top of that, Marten lost an elk! His javelin struck a pine branch, and the bull ran off across the ice. Marten was left behind in the soft snow. If only there had been a crust! No real crust last winter, not ever.

"We lost some other chances too, and were running out of food. There was nothing left but to turn to the Guardians. Helleborine advised us to sacrifice the last of our meat to them and to pray for better hunting."

Tiger fell silent for a while. Standing beside each other, he and Whitespear were paddling the raft across the channel. In his inner eye there was a clear picture of that winter scene and the gathering on the south shore of the island. He saw the great snow-clad expanse of sea-ice. He saw the sacrificial pyre and the people thronged around it, all talking excitedly about hunting parties inland and sealing expeditions to the isle of Morningland, far out in the sea. And there, among the voluble, gesticulating Whites, was the silent figure of Baywillow, brown-eyed and brown-haired, now very frail and thin. He was looking from one to another, sometimes raising a hand to his head where the scar of his injury stood out like a white parting, and occasionally giving a slight smile. People cared for him: he was forever receiving a friendly pat on the shoulder or a brief caress on his arm. He seemed to understand all that was said, but his only response was that little secretive smile.

Tiger gave him his firing gear: the firestone, the flint, and some dry reed-tops for tinder. Baywillow understood at once and gave him a grateful look. He fumbled a little but soon had the tinder on fire, and the flames spread rapidly. Veyde now stepped up, holding a slice of meat in each hand. She raised them above her head and uttered a prayer to all the Guardians to have mercy upon them and to give them a sign. The fire was roaring. She threw one piece of meat into the flames. "To the Guardians of the elk, the mammoth, and all four-legged beasts!" she said. Then the other: "To the Guardians of the seal and all the fish in the sea!"

"A sign!" repeated the people in unison.

The fire crackled and sent out a shower of sparks. Some of the dry reeds on the shore went up in flames. Was it a sign? All were silent and expectant. They nudged each other, but no one dared speak. A great pillar of smoke was rising from the fire.

"Then," said Tiger, "somebody cried out and pointed to the sky. We saw the smoke backing up and gathering in a cloud just above us, and spreading out to the sides. The smoke of our sacrifice to the Guardians! Invisible and malignant, some powerful spirit was checking its rise. The cloud grew out on all sides, dimming the sun.

"We were struck by terror. The Powers were showing their displeasure: they refused our offering. We had fallen into disgrace. The smoke-cloud grew ever wider and denser. A dark shadow spread over us. The sun was gone: it was hiding its face from us! Many of us threw ourselves on the ground; others just stared, paralyzed by fright. Somebody wailed, and others started to gabble.

"I looked at Baywillow: it was he who had kindled the fire. He looked back at me gravely, earnestly, and I thought there was a message in his eyes. He came over to me and moved his lips as if to speak, but remained mute. He sighed, gripped my arm briefly, then turned around and went—home, I thought. That was the last time I saw him."

Tiger fell silent again. He was filled by memories of his half-brother, with whom he had shared so many adventures, dangers, joys. The raft grounded on the shore of Veyde's Island just as the rising sun shone out over the forest edge to the northeast. Silent and brooding, Whitespear followed Tiger along the track to the village. Behind him came Kite, who now felt herself a stranger and sorely confused: her mission had come to nought. Humble Heather brought up the rear, chewing his resin and darting curious glances around him. He had never been in the islands before.

Tiger stopped suddenly.

"He had gone away across the ice," he said. "We saw his tracks next day. But well before that, the Guardians sent us a wind that swept away the smoke-cloud, and we were so relieved that nobody remembered Baywillow. When at last we started to follow his tracks, the Guardians sent a blizzard to blot them out. Thus we knew that Baywillow had acted upon their will when he left."

Whitespear had stopped too. For a moment he stood still. Then he raised his clenched fists to the treetops, aflame in the morning sun.

"Then the Powers are to blame! They tricked him as they did me! False and faithless are the Powers, a mockery they

make of your life and your honor! Their eye is the eye of the
viper, their heart is the heart of the blizzard, their head is the
laughing head of the hyena! Damnation to them! *My knife in
their eye, my spear in their heart, my axe in their head!*"

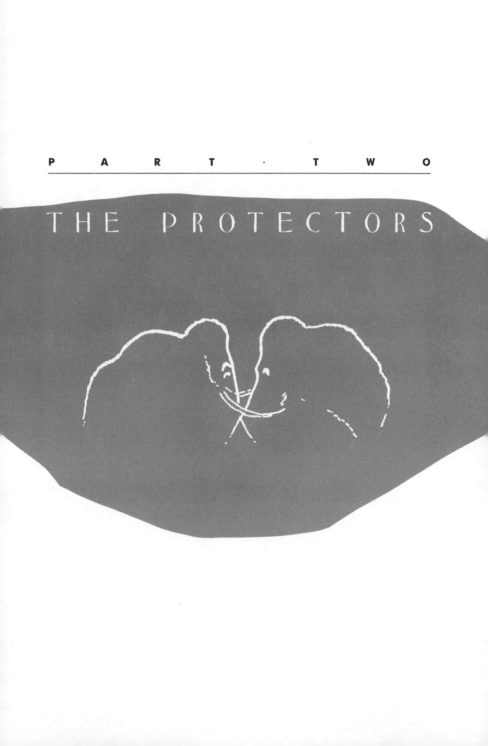

PART · TWO

THE PROTECTORS

THE · POWERS

"**A**re the Powers good or evil, Oriole? When I was a child I saw the Guardians once. I knew then that they cared. They made themselves known, let themselves be seen.

"Now they had betrayed me. They had sent Siskin to me and made me fail in my quest to find a healer for Baywillow. Thus cruelly they played with me, and I could only see my wrongs.

"I had a sister once, Centaury by name. She was one of the Browns—her mother was Miss Silverweed, a White woman, and she was Baywillow's daughter, but she was sired by Tiger like myself. Miss Silverweed was killed in the Shelk feud, long before I was born. I remember Centaury from my childhood. She was different from us, like a stranger looking for her rightful place. Once I heard her wailing: Hind told me that she was crying for her mother, whom she had never known. She was kind to me, but I always felt that she was thinking of something else. Her mother had been like that too, Tiger said.

"There was a rock pool she was fond of. You could lie on a ledge above it and look down into the water, and there you would see a picture of yourself and the sky and the birds. She could lie there for half a day, but not just to look at herself or to plait her hair. She looked far down and far away. When you spoke to her, she did not look into your eyes but to the side of you, or at your mouth, as if she expected something to jump out of it. Did she look for spirits, for the Powers?

"Twice she went away. The first time, she came back a moon later with a bad scar across her brow. She would not tell how she got it but just said that she had hacked herself about. The second time, she did not come back. We lost her tracks on the ice: the wind had swept it free of snow. In my thoughts she had been taken to the bottom of the sea, and I could see her down there, looking up to the mirror of its surface. Maybe that was where she wanted to be. Long afterwards, Baywillow said, 'Centaury is not coming back.'

"Why did she go? Why didn't she want to stay with us any more? Maybe it was because of Hind. She never was her child. They were like strangers to each other. Many summers later Avens told me that she knew Centaury's secret, but she did not say what it was.

"Now Baywillow was gone like his firstborn child. Maybe he was down there too, at her side. But this time it was my fault. And that was why I turned against the Powers and cursed them, and swore never again to fail.

"Oh, the Powers have two faces, like Shelk: one that is evil and one that is good. They strike with one hand and they give with the other. The Powers are ancient—older than everything in the world. The world and all the things that are in it arose out of their dreams. They have seen all, tasted all, heard all, smelled all. They are great in wisdom.

They are neither good nor evil. If you help yourself, it may be that they will help you. If you do not help yourself, it may be that they will destroy you. What remains to you is to walk your own road and keep faith with those who trust you. Then the Powers become powerless. They may still destroy you, but never your peace of mind and your honor."

HIND

"The Whites are good people," said Hind, "but they are very ignorant about some things. The way they go around in the summer, stark naked . . . I tell you I didn't believe my eyes when I first came here! The women flaunting their sex and tits for anybody to see—not that they are much to look at, to my mind. I'm glad you don't take after them, my dear Kite. Still, they are polite and considerate, I'll give them that. Some of the men are quite fine-looking, once you get used to their faces. And of course, old Silverbirch was a dear, he really was. He tried so hard to speak a real language. Yes, you must not judge the Whites by their appearance."

"Oh, I don't," said Kite. "They do look peculiar, but my father told me that we have much to learn from their shamans, or healers, as they call them."

"Is that so?" said Hind, somewhat surprised. "I daresay. But they are very childish in some things. Of course, they are splendid hunters, really splendid. Never any difficulty about food. Oh, they are generous to a degree. But sometimes . . . oh, sometimes I long to be back among our own people! The Whites have no arts—have you heard them sing, Kite? It is terrible, like the laughing of a hyena! They can only speak their own jabbering language. And they have no pictures." Her eyes suddenly filled with tears. "Dear Baywillow could make pictures—not like Tiger, but pictures—and he was, he *was,* a miracle to the Whites!"

Hind and Kite were alone on the highest point of the island, a rock platform rising well over the treetops. Kite gathered that Hind had something to tell her and probably did not wish to be overheard. There was a dazzling view of the sea to the south, glittering in the afternoon sun. This was still a novelty to Kite, who would gaze at it with great wonder. Beside them the Sun Pillar raked into the sky, graven with innumerable animal pictures. It was Tiger's work, Hind had told her, and she had pointed with pride to the likenesses of a shelk and a black tiger. "You can see that Shelk and Tiger loved each other in the end," she had said.

She handed Kite a small wineskin that she had brought along, and the girl took a sip. She was truly astounded and immediately took a second one.

"Hind," she said, "this is something I have never tasted before. My father makes wine, but nothing like this. If this is your work, you must be greatly beloved by the Guardians."

Hind smiled. "I am very happy about your coming here, Kite," she said. "You know enough to appreciate a good thing. That's where we Blacks differ from the Whites. They do not understand about wine. Yet it is one of the supreme gifts of the Guardians. It is for the sake of the wine that they let the berries ripen on the moor and the shore meadow, in the forest and the glade. Where I came from we had great repute as winemakers, and I learned the art from my mother. Well I remember how her art was extolled by our people, and by everybody who visited us at Big Lake!"

"You must teach me, Hind. I have some wine-lore from my father, but he mostly brews shaman wine."

"That I know nothing about. But I do know that the spirit of the wine is willful and full of tricks. You have to approach him with clean hands and a clean heart, or he may give you a potion as bitter as the venom of the adder."

"That is so. The best thing for raising him is a small skin of old wine."

"Yes," said Hind, "but his sleep is deep and he can only be roused by the sweetest of the berries. To begin with, you can feed him with strawberries or raspberries, unless you are using sap or honey. Yes, even the insipid cornel berry may stir him to life. The bilberry, never. And it is a good thing to start with an old wine, as you say, or you may get one of his naughty brothers! Still, once you have raised him, he will make himself known: you will have a frothing, foaming mash. Then, and only then, can you start on your big brew. Now he will devour the bilberry, and it will become his blood: he will give you the black wine. Yes, I'll teach you, Kite, and we'll make wine together!

"Now," she went on eagerly, "when the spirit is great and powerful, is the time to add to the brew. Use the pith of the rosebay and the juice of the angelica to increase the quantity and improve the taste. Now is the time for the hoard of golden cloudberry and purple whortleberry. Do you wish to impart healing powers to the wine? Then add yarrow and mint, valerian and sweet gale. All the time, the wine is advancing, and its spirit is at the peak of his strength. At this time you can even add lingonberry, but do so sparingly and carefully. Used in the right way it adds to the vigor of the spirit, but too much will thin the brew and give it an unpleasant tang."

Timidly, Kite interposed, "I remember one spring when

my father started a wine on last year's lingonberries. Together with birch sap, of course."

Hind nodded eagerly. "Yes. I was going to say that. Win-
tering makes the lingonberry mellow enough for the spirit
of the wine, and the cranberry too." Now she lowered her
voice mysteriously: "I have saved the best to the last. Out in
the skerries grows yet another berry, which I came to know
only after I had moved here. It is not found inland at all. It is
the berry of the sea-buckthorn, and its potency is the greatest
of all! You have to journey to the outer islands—there, and
there"—she pointed seaward—"and you will find that its
Guardian has given it a tremendous defense! When you harvest it, you leave one drop of your blood on every branch.
Add the sea-buckthorn to your wine and its glory will be
such that your torn hands will be forgotten. You will have a
potion such as the Guardians themselves would esteem, and
the happy smiles of your people will be your reward!"

She was lost in happy reverie for a while. Then her expression changed: "But here it is no use—no one but Tiger to
appreciate what I do. And now you and Whitespear, of
course. Dear Baywillow liked my wine too, and now he's
gone . . . The Whites don't understand. I think they feel it's
some kind of poison. That woman Veyde is no better, and
her brood never had any time for me, though they speak our
tongue. Oh, Kite, I've been so lonesome! Never a woman to
speak to. I thank the Powers that Whitespear chose you!
Always I feared that he would take up with a Troll b—I
mean a White girl."

She peered down among the trees uneasily. "Is there
somebody there? I thought I saw something moving."

Kite, too, had seen a glimpse of a feral, timid figure down
there, secretive and silent like the spirit of the woods. She
laughed.

"It's Heather. He always follows me around."

"Why?" asked Hind suspiciously. "Does he have a claim
on you?"

"No. I think he wants to protect me. As you see, he's being tactful. He won't intrude. Besides, he doesn't understand what we say."

"I see." Hind dismissed Heather with a shrug. "It is really Whitespear who worries me: he's changed. What's wrong with him, Kite?"

"Hind, he frightens me! He curses the Powers!" Kite gave a shiver. "I'm afraid that—that the way he's going on, Shelk will turn against him."

"He won't do that! I can't believe he will! If it is really true that Shelk is now the one who governs our destiny, then he cannot turn against Hind's last child alive! I should know: I was Shelk's woman once."

"You!" cried Kite, awestruck. She looked with amazement at the older woman. There she was, sitting right beside her, and she had been Shelk's woman! She tried to imagine what Hind had looked like, all those winters ago. "You must have been very beautiful," she said.

Hind laughed, a little harshly. "Perhaps. Yes, I have no fear of Shelk any more. He has had his revenge. Did you not know? Dear Baywillow—it was he who killed Shelk the Destroyer and that is why he went away. He had no speech, he couldn't tell me, but I saw it in his eyes. The curse was on Baywillow and on him only, and he knew it. He left us to make us free. Do you see now?"

She raised her arms as if in prayer. "Shelk has robbed me of almost everything. He took three of my children. Now he has taken Baywillow. Tiger was to be my man; he took him away and gave him to that woman Veyde. Yet I have had Tiger back, and have him still. He is the father of my children, the three who died and the one who lives. That is what I have left, and Shelk shall not have that. You must help me, Kite. You have the wisdom of the shamans, young as you are. You know the mysteries, you know how to reach the Powers. Use your knowledge, use your strength, stand by me and Whitespear!"

. . .

Siskin came back to Whitespear during those days of early
spring at Veyde's Island. He carried her picture within him
whatever he did, whether he went hunting or fishing. Soon
he kept away from the others, walking alone on the shore,
trying to talk to her. It always ended with her ghostly image
turning against him, crouching viciously and ordering him
to go away.

Kite sometimes followed him at a distance. She thought
he was getting sparer and thinner every day.

One day he found a big polished piece of driftwood. The
first picture he made was Siskin's eyes, always unfathomable. He drew many pairs of eyes until he thought he had
them right. Then he threw away the piece of driftwood and
started on another. He filled it with new pictures: the long
contour of her back, many times, always more beautiful,
more real. On other pieces of wood he carved other parts of
her body. He dismembered her image and engraved the bits
into the wood, her limbs, her sex, her neck, the tresses of
her hair. Day after day he worked, alone, on the shore.

Kite watched him covertly. She had picked up some of the
pictures and thought she knew what he was doing. She was
deeply troubled now. I could have told him, she thought, I
could have explained. I could have sent him back to Siskin.

Whitespear felt that he was in the grip of the Powers. They
held him fast and would give him no peace unless he finished
his work. But now, as he toiled, it seemed that with every
picture he made, the image of Siskin grew fainter in his
mind. She was fading away.

The time came when he was empty. In that moment the
Powers relinquished their grip. He rose uncertainly and
looked out to sea. The sun was setting behind the islands and
a single streak of cloud burned over the horizon. Gulls passed
overhead, flying to their nests. The bay was dotted with

eider ducks, and he became aware of their friendly murmuring. Everything was new, strange, unknown. His widened nostrils took in the scent of the evening, of the sea, of early spring—drying mud, tender herbs.

He was holding something in his hand. What could it be? A piece of elk antler. There was a picture on it: a woman. He must have made it but he could not remember doing so. Idly, he wondered whom it represented. He started to walk homeward. A blackbird warbled in the wood.

The evening was warm and dusk was gathering. Kite, who had been watching Whitespear, was diverted by the unexpected sight of a strange animal crawling along in the moss. She stared at it incredulously. She had never seen a toad and did not know what it was. She knew the small brown frogs of Swidden Moor; maybe this was a frog with a disease that had caused it to swell up and develop hideous warts all over. Then she saw another, and suddenly realized that the wood was full of them. There was a big fat one carrying another on its back! Her reason told her that this was a new kind of frog, and she playfully coined a name for it: "Troll frog."

The creatures were all going in the same direction, slowly and painfully. She went along with them and saw that they were headed for a tarn in which some of their number were already swimming around.

Whitespear, walking along the shore, became aware of Kite beside the tarn. The sight of her filled the emptiness within him. Coming closer, he stopped at arm's length and handed her the picture. She looked at it wonderingly.

"Who is it?" she asked. "Siskin?"

"No. It is you."

Moving toward her, he stepped right on a toad, and slipped and fell, pulling her down with him. They burst out laughing as they grabbed each other. "It's you!" he repeated. "Yes!" she said. "Yes, yes! You stepped on a Troll frog, Whitespear!" "It was a toad," he said. "Oh, *that's* what it

is?" she said. "Poor old toad!" he said. "Blessed old toad!"
she said, and they laughed again.

She cried out when he penetrated her, drawing blood. In
the wood, Heather made an involuntary movement. Then
he settled down contentedly, chewing his resin. Everything
was as it should be. His goddess had made her choice. The
sounds now told him that she was having a good time.
Heather lay down on his back in the moss and grinned with
satisfaction.

.   .   .

That was the beginning of a new life for Kite. In her first
moments of despair, she had thought that her journey had
been in vain. Now, she had been received with love by Hind,
and had become Whitespear's woman. But she had gained
even more, and Veyde told her so.

"We need you," she said. "We have had no healer since
Mister Helleborine left us last winter, and Miss Bracken with
him. They went to Blue Lake together, and no one knows if
she is coming back."

Kite was aware of the tension between Hind and Veyde.
Hind spoke with disdain of the White woman; Veyde, for
her part, rarely affected to take any notice of Hind. With
Kite, on the other hand, she was friendly from the start, and
took her out to show her the island. "You must learn to
know our land: let me show you. All the signs are good for
the summer. A swan pair is nesting in the reeds on the west
shore, and the long-tailed duck rested here in great numbers
earlier in the spring."

Kite remembered what Whitespear had told her about
these, the two holy birds of the island people. They even had
their own constellations among the stars: he had pointed
them out. They were the same that the Blacks called the
Mammoth and the Mammoth Spear, and they trailed each
other forever around the North Star. To the Whites, they

were the sacred birds, the Great Swan that laid the World
Egg, and the singing duck that came when the year turned
from cold to warm. It was all very difficult to understand—
who was right, the Blacks or the Whites? Maybe both. The
Whites, Kite reflected, surely had great wisdom.

She cast a thoughtful glance at the White woman by her
side. Veyde moved bouncingly, almost as if she were dancing, in an excess of strength and exuberance. Compared with
her, the other Whites seemed almost languid, yet they were
very different on the hunt, Whitespear had told her. Kite
thought, My people would have called her a Troll bitch. She
felt suddenly chilled. Who was this being? She was powerful
enough to rend her, Kite, apart in a single effort. But Harrier's teaching came to her aid. "Thus says Shelk," her father
had said, "the Whites wish us no harm. When you see them
for the first time, you think they are the people of the nether
earth, called forth to destroy us. But they are wise and kind,
wiser and kinder than the Blacks. Only the ignorant despise
them; the wise one seeks their friendship. There are many
things to learn from them. Yea, let White and Black meet
and learn from each other in all times to come."

Impulsively, Kite said, "I seek your friendship, Miss
Veyde."

The White woman grinned. "You speak our tongue very
well. I cannot speak the bird-talk like you! You Blacks talk
so beautifully and quickly, just like birds."

"I want to learn your language properly. It is hard."

"It sounds funny sometimes when you speak it," Veyde
admitted with a laugh. "It was the same with Tiger when he
came here. Then he could not say a thing. But you—you
come here and speak so that we understand. It is very courteous of you." She passed her hand over her eyes.

Suddenly she stopped and gripped Kite's arm. "Listen,
Miss Kite!"

Kite had heard the bird, too. She recognized it from its

manner of singing rather than from the song itself: strong,
sonorous phrases, repeated two or three times. "I know the
bird but I do not know your name for it." Veyde, obviously
very happy, told her the White name for the song thrush,
and added, "We do not have him every summer, you know.
This is a good sign. Listen to him now! He is making fun of
the redshank. He is telling us that he belongs here." Veyde
danced around and clapped her hands. She was right; Kite
could hear the thrush mimicking the sad whistle of the redshank. "He is greeting you, Miss Kite. It will be a good
summer."

Kite smiled. "You are not like the other Whites," she said.
"They arc so slow and careful. As if they were afraid of—of
breaking something. You are different. So—so merry."

"Oh, they all say that. Old Silverbirch used to scold me.
Miss Veyde, he said, you behave in a most unseemly manner. I do not understand the youth of today." Veyde made a
face and burst into laughter. They had reached a narrow
channel separating Veyde's Island from the next island to the
west. "Look at this, Miss Kite. My great-great-great-
grandmother—she was called Miss Cowslip daughter of
Whortleberry—well, she swam across here when her life was
in danger. A bear was after her, a mother with her cub. And
she had to swim, you see? But now"—Veyde stepped into
the water—"now I can wade across. The water is going
away, very slowly, from generation to generation. That is
the way it is. All things change, nothing remains the same.
We know, we Whites: we know all about the old times and
the old people, about the beginnings of time, when there
were no Blacks."

"All things change," Kite repeated thoughtfully.

"All things change, all things live. The earth, the stones,
the sea. Their life is very slow, very patient: they draw one
breath a day. But of course you know all this, Miss Kite, for
you are very wise."

. . .

Kite was altogether happy during her first summer on Veyde's Island. She was curious and eager to learn, and her quick brain retained everything. The sea and the islands were new to her, for she had grown up inland. She was much impressed by the Whites' sureness and competence in their world, so different from her own, while at the same time their circumspect and courteous ways filled her with amused wonder. Most of all, she was entranced by their reverence for the birds, their rich bird-lore, and their belief in an after-life in bird guise. She tried to combine that with the Shelk-worship she had learned from her father, and it puzzled her a great deal. Also, though the birds were holy to the Whites, that did not deter them from hunting woodfowl and collecting eggs from the nests of the eider and merganser ducks. Never more than three eggs, though, for three was the holy number. Three were the gulls: the smaller black-backed one, the common gull with its white brow, and the great black-winged bird of the open sea. Three were the terns: the silver-winged arctic tern, the common tern, and the giant tern with its raucous voice. Three were the forest trees: the aspen, the birch, and the pine. Again, the growing angelica made three green eggs, and out of the last one burst the flowers.

She wanted to make friends of Whitespear's brown siblings, the children of Tiger and Veyde. She succeeded in part only. Marten, the great hunter, was aloof: he looked at her, friendly but absent-minded, and went his own ways. His eye and ear seemed always to be open to things too far away or too small to be seen or heard by others. Of late he had been joined by his youngest sister, Gale, now very tall and rather like him, a solitary, boyish huntress. Those two made long journeys, returning with few words but lots of game. To-

wards autumn they vanished and did not return. A few—
but only a few—knew that they had been reached by Avens's
message: *Come and join us!* And those few did not tell.

With Marigold, Kite had nothing in common. She found
the big, buxom woman childish and suspected that she was
jealous for Whitespear's sake. But Mullein, who was close to
Kite herself in age, became a friend. Soon she was the confi-
dante to whom Kite would talk freely about her ambitions
and her complicated religious speculations. The Brown girl
was a patient listener. She herself was a slow talker, often
beset by fits of stuttering, which made her laugh. Yet it was
with her help that Kite found her ideas untangled and forming a coherent whole of beliefs and concepts. She created a
transcendental image of Shelk as the Guardian of birds—
why, Harrier had told her of Shelk's soul-bird, the talking
raven who would perch on his outstretched hand. Yes, that
must be right, Mullein nodded, and Kite rejoiced. So much
to tell Harrier! How proud he would be of all her newfound
wisdom!

Then, towards the end of summer, came surfeit. Suddenly, Kite found herself utterly bored by the Whites. She
looked critically at their big faces and squat bodies. She
found their courtesies exaggerated and their gestures, hands
over eyes, irritating. The moment came one evening when
the Whites had got together for one of their favorite pas-
times, storytelling. The stories, which were usually of their
own forebears and their deeds in bygone times, often turned
into songs, sometimes wordless. The song seemed to grope
and grow like water collecting in a rock pool in the rain,
overflowing, seeking its way down in a winding, increasing
runnel; it would be taken up now by one, now by another,
with a great chorus in which everybody joined. The song
was never the same from one time to the next; it was always
created anew, and in its ceaseless flow everybody found
communion and sharing—with each other, with those who

had gone, with those who were to come. During earlier singing evenings, Kite had been enchanted by the Whites' solemn joy and the visionary wonder in their faces. Now she only felt alien. She looked around: there were Tiger and Whitespear, not singing, but listening and smiling. Marigold and Mullein were singing and rocking with the music. Hind was not there. Kite rose and went to look for her, and after much searching found her crouched in a narrow fissure, her hands over her ears. Kite kneeled down at her side, and Hind took her in her arms. They knew themselves to be outcasts, unbearably, and sought comfort in each other's company.

Then one of them got the idea of paddling to another island to collect buckthorn berries. Suddenly all was different. They giggled like small girls as they stole down to the shore and set out in a coracle. It was twilight and the waters were still when they reached the skerry, where they planned to spend the night. In the distance they could see the fire on the shore of Veyde's Island and its reflection in the swell, like a steadily dripping, glowing liquid. Broken notes of the song reached them, almost drowned in the incessant chirping of the crickets.

They sat down on the west side, wrapped in skins, their backs to Veyde's Island. Before them burned the last red glow of the dying day and just above it curled the moon like the chip from an axe-stroke. A soft night-breeze brought with it the fragrance of autumn woods and wetlands from inland.

Kite told of her anxiety for Whitespear. He had turned against the Powers and would not share her faith. Yet she hoped that he would change his mind. Hind agreed, but warned Kite to tread carefully. He would not be won over by magpie prattle.

Now they heard a light splashing and scraping: somebody else was coming ashore. Kite laughed. "It's Heather. He gets uneasy as soon as I go away."

He kept at a respectful distance, though. Kite could just discern him, reclining on a tree-trunk, chewing his resin, silent and patient, true to his self-assumed duty, protecting his goddess against all dangers.

JAY

The c h a n g e of the seasons on Veyde's Island was the same as on Swidden Moor, but to Kite there was a difference. Out here the autumn was harder to stand. It wasn't just that the days grew shorter; it was the darkness, so dense, so brooding. Although a snowfall would brighten the scene for a day or two, the snow would melt as quickly as it came, and all the time the sea remained a vast blackness. Even when there was a lasting snow-cover, the sea stayed ice-free, and so the world became darker and darker as if passing into endless night. And Kite found the howling of the wind and the assault of the waves far more frightening than at Horn Lake. She felt numbed by the uproar, which seemed never to end, and even in the snug winter house into which she and Whitespear had moved, it was as if she felt constantly buffeted.

The islanders couldn't care less. During the brief hours of daylight they would bring down their game with unfailing skill: horse and elk were easy to track in the melting snow. But their great moment came one day when mammoths were sighted on the mainland. By raft and boat they made their way across the sound, in a vicious gale with rapidly thickening snowfall, and went to the traditional mammoth pit. It had served for generations, and innumerable mammoths had been taken in it over the years. Now some repairs were necessary; caved-in edges were rebuilt, and the pointed pole at the bottom had to be inspected. Meanwhile, Veyde took a group of hunters to the mammoths.

In the early dusk of evening, torches were kindled. Screaming like demented spirits, the hunters rushed at the mammoths. The animals dispersed in a panic, and the hunters started to drive the young bull that Veyde had chosen towards the forest and the mammoth pit. The torches whirled and flared in the driving snow, the yelling figures appeared now here, now there, forcing the mammoth ever closer to its doom, and in the end the terrified giant crashed into the pit, with a last desperate trumpeting, and was impaled.

A moon-quarter later came the cold, still morning when Kite experienced the mystery of the sea becoming icebound. The sun glared frostily in the mirror of the ice: the world brightened, the sun was turning back, and everything suddenly became serene and peaceful as if all the turmoil of autumn had been muffled by the snow.

So the winter passed, and then, after several moons, spring was upon them, with the breaking up of the ice and the return of the seafowl in endless multitudes.

Long ago, Kite had reconciled herself to the Whites. No longer did she see them as a uniform crowd; they had become individuals to her, and she knew that beneath the courteous surface they all carried their own loves and hates. For herself, she had known friendship and honor. As a healer, she had been successful, though to tell the truth, she wasn't often needed. Besides a broken bone or two, the commonest ailment was that constant scourge of the Whites, the tapeworm.

But in one regard she felt a failure. Here it was, her second summer on the island, and she was still childless. After much soul-searching she turned to Heather.

"Mister Heather, my highest wish is to give Mister Whitespear a son. Among you Whites there is a custom that a childless man will ask his brother to help him out. Whitespear's brother, though, died many years ago. You, Mister Heather, are my hope. Will you help me? You already have a child with your woman, Miss Orache."

Heather was visibly taken aback. "Miss Kite, I want to do all I can for you, but that is impossible."

"Why?"

He scratched his head and pulled his hands over his eyes. "It is like this," he started and stopped, searching for words. "With Miss Orache, it is fun. She jumps at me or I at her. We roll around and we laugh. We rub against each other and have a good time." He laughed at his memories, and Kite laughed too. She found his artless description, in the circumstantial language of the Whites, quite irresistible.

"Yes," she said, "I know! But what about me?"

Once more, Heather passed his hands over his eyes. "You, Miss Kite, are a goddess. You are my goddess. I cannot dream of a union with you."

"I do not understand."

"It is so, anyway. And then, you are not just a goddess; you are a child, too. Did you not know? You have the faces of children, all of you Blacks. No, no, it is impossible."

Kite stared unseeing at the sea. Her second summer on Veyde's Island was running out, and she wanted a son. Why did the Powers deny her this? Was it because of Whitespear? He had defied them. And yet he had engraved a picture in Shelk's honor once. He even had the makings of a shaman:

Harrier himself said so. She shook her head and tears burned in her eyes.

"I can help others; I cannot help myself. What should I do, Mister Heather?"

"I have heard that too, about healers helping others but not themselves. But there is talk here of a great healer, Mister Helleborine. He was here once, but he returned home again. Maybe if you were to seek him out, Miss Kite . . ."

Kite drew a deep breath. Suddenly, an old dream had come to life within her. Yes! All too long she had been living from day to day, she who had wanted to become a great shaman and learn from the White healers. She decided then and there: she was going to Helleborine. "Where does he live?" she asked.

Heather could not say. But Whitespear thought he knew. Helleborine, he said, was the healer of Blue Lake; and he himself was ready to go to Blue Lake with Kite, for he too wanted a child. He blamed Kite's barrenness on the Powers: maybe Helleborine could outwit them. His heart warmed at his memory of the old man with the kind blue eyes.

"You mustn't defy the Powers," said Kite.

"I never did them any harm," Whitespear answered. "The guilt is theirs. And here we have prospered, except for this. Anyway, let's make the journey, Kite."

"Maybe Shelk will give you a sign," said Kite hopefully.

So they departed together once more, in late summer this time. And Heather came along, making three of them as before: wherever Kite went, he would go too. They set out at dawn, when the full moon was setting.

· · ·

"I wondered what they'd do to us," Whitespear told Oriole. "The last time I went to Blue Lake, the Browns were far from friendly. And what did they think of Goshawk's death? As it turned out, though, I needn't have worried. The village was abandoned. Down at the lakeshore, the summer tents were gone, and the winter houses were empty. Indeed, most of the roofs had caved in.

"It had been abandoned, like Big Lake Village, but for a very different reason, as I was later to know. Big Lake was abandoned because everybody was killed—by Heather and his tribe. With Blue Lake, it was different. As I told you, almost everybody there was Brown, and they had all gone away at the call to arms: the call of Avens. Of course, we knew nothing about that.

"So, what to do? We didn't like the idea of turning back. In the end we decided to go on to Swidden Moor. Maybe Harrier, Kite's father, would be able to help us. The journey, we thought, would be fine: it was a good time for game.

"Kite, I could see, was dejected. She had looked forward to meeting Helleborine, the great healer. On the other hand, Swidden Moor was the home of her childhood, and she agreed readily enough.

"We had good hunting, and plenty of berries and mushrooms in the forest. On the fourth day out, Heather stopped and held his hand aloft. He was sniffing into the wind. 'I smell mammoth,' he said.

"Yes, Oriole, the Whites have a very sharp nose. I tried my best, and thought I felt the ghost of a smell. Heather was right. 'It is early in the season for mammoth,' I said.

"Heather agreed. 'They are early sometimes,' he said. 'Loners, mostly.'

"Which is quite true, as you know. Of course, this put ideas into my head. A loner meant a big bull. Dangerous, but rewarding, if the Guardian so wills. I knew that Heather was a brave and skilled hunter. If we could steer the mammoth into an ambush, we might be able to bag him, just between the three of us.

"Kite was eager too. 'He is in front of us, so we'll lose nothing by tracking him,' she said.

"We were on top of a hill, looking at the land in front. I felt the light west wind on my cheeks. Heather extended his arm. 'Over there,' he said. 'We may see him from the next esker.'

"So we ran down into the valley and across the marsh, and worked uphill. Here the pines grew sparsely, and there were young birches everywhere. You could see there had been a forest fire, summers ago. Towards the crest we moved cautiously, taking cover behind the young trees and peeping out between the branches.

"It was not one mammoth, but two. They were facing each other and I hardly dared believe my eyes, for one of them was Singletusk himself. The other one was big too, but nothing like Singletusk. I think they had just met. They took no notice of us. They held their trunks straight down, and saw only each other. You could hear the crack when the tusks made contact.

"They pushed at each other, but Singletusk was the stronger, and the other one tottered. That was all that was needed. He pulled out right away. He rushed backward, hesitated for a breath, then turned tail and ran away. Singletusk remained standing, looking very avuncular: There, I've given the youngster a lesson. At a safe distance, the other one slowed down and started to amble away as if nothing had happened. He seemed to be saying, 'That was only in fun, and now I have other things to do.' I had to smile, and I heard Kite tittering.

"It was the first time I saw Singletusk fighting—but not the last.

"As soon as I clapped eyes on him, I knew that he was a messenger of the Guardians. I've never had any trouble with them: they have always been on my side, unlike some other Powers. Singletusk and I had a compact, and he would show the way. Now all we had to do was follow him. He would be our guide.

"He went south. We kept in touch by walking downwind from him. Heather's nose served us well, and sometimes we had a glimpse of Singletusk from a hilltop. Always the sight moved me deeply, and images would arise within me: Singletusk, immense and lonely, invincible, the biggest and strongest of them all—and yet it had been vouchsafed me to see him in one moment of weakness. I felt very close to him.

"We tracked him that day and the next. In the evening we spied the smoke of a campfire. And there he left us, and went his own ways."

.   .   .

The dusk was already gathering when they reached the camp. Whitespear called out at a distance, and they saw two men get to their feet. They were gripping their spears, but when Whitespear appeared in the firelight with his hands raised, they put them away.

"Jay!" Whitespear cried out, for he had recognized the trader. "Do you remember me?"

"Whitespear, the artist from Veyde's Island," said Jay, smiling broadly. "I'm not likely to forget you. Is that your woman? But where ever did you dig up that Troll ox? By the Black Hill, these are curious times, and you get some curious company too."

They embraced, and Whitespear said, "The Guardians have brought us to you. But why are you here, Jay? This is the time of the Summer Meet, isn't it? It's hardly two quarters since the full moon."

Jay's hands fluttered in a gesture of exasperation. "There was no Meet. There are evil powers in the woods down North, Whitespear. Nobody dares go there any more. They say that there are Brown wolfmen abroad. More than one has been killed by them. That's why you find me here with most of my goods untraded. Ah, the long voyage has been all in vain this summer! Yes, Whitespear, these are strange

times. Here you are at my campfire, and I hardly have even
the shank of a vixen to offer you."

Whitespear turned to Heather and spoke to him in the
White language, and Heather put down his great pack. "We
have enough for all of us, Jay, and I want you to drink a
hornful of the black wine with us."

While Kite and Heather prepared the little feast, Whitespear took a furtive look at the trader. He was much the
same as he had been two summers ago, but there was a
sprinkling of grey in his hair and beard, which gave him a
certain dignity. Why the Guardians had led them to him was
hard to understand. What should he tell him? It would be
artless to blurt out his errand right away. Better talk of other
things and let him sample Hind's black wine.

Jay smacked his lips. "This is a drink for the Guardians to
enjoy," he said.

"So no one turned up at the larch grove?" asked Whitespear.

"Well, so I was told. I traveled north by way of Falcon
Hill and Swidden Moor, and they warned me not to go any
farther. No one is safe in the North, the wolfmen are lurking
everywhere. I'm not a coward, and Cuckoo, my helper, is a
good man—but what's the use of going to the Meet if nobody else is coming? So we thought we'd take the eastern
route back and see what we could trade on the way. That's
why we are here: we are going back home, back to
Birchneck Village in the Land of Flints."

"And have you traded anything?"

"Hardly anything. Nobody has the time or cares to trade
when the forest is full of dangers. I'll finish up by toting
most of my things back home!" Jay took another swallow
and gave the horn to Cuckoo, a tall young man who looked
bashful and sat well to one side.

During the meal, Jay kept looking curiously at Heather,
who ate quickly and went back to chewing his resin. Noting
this, Whitespear briefly told how they had found him. The

trader listened attentively, and Whitespear saw that he was storing the narrative in his memory: such news would make him welcome in every village.

Now Jay cast a searching glance at Whitespear. "You say that the Guardians have led you to me. Do you have any goods to trade? Your handiwork is the most precious of all. There is no artist in the Land of Flints to measure up to you."

"I might have," said Whitespear carefully. He steeled himself and went on in a light tone, "Do you have a remedy for childlessness?"

"Ah!" said Jay, his hands flapping like wings in the light of the fire. "Trust me, my dear friend. I have been able to help many couples, from Birchneck to Big Lake. By the Black Hill, the Guardians did bring you to the right place!"

Cuckoo rose to put more fuel on the fire, then withdrew tactfully. Kite sat motionless, looking at Jay from beneath her fringe. The trader cast a quick glance at her, seemed encouraged by what he saw, and continued, "Did you ever hear about the thunderbolt, Whitespear?"

"The thunderbolt? You mean the lightning and the rumble? There is a flash, you hear a peal, and that's all. They say it's the utterance of the Guardian of the mammoth, the fire from his eye."

"And they are right. But we from the South, from the Land of Flints, know more about this than other people. Because, you see, the Guardian gives us the bolt itself. Oh, not always, far from it! Yet sometimes the Guardians choose a man to find the bolt—the one that fell to the ground. And in that bolt, all the male power is vested."

Kite, who had been silent, spoke for the first time: "I have heard of it. Are you telling us, Jay, that you have a thunderbolt with you?"

"Yes, my child," said the trader in a fatherly manner, "I do indeed. What's more, my bolt is special. Most of them are found on the ground. But sometimes you find one in a tree, in the place where the lightning split it, and that bolt is the most powerful of them all. It's a tree-bolt like that that I have here, and it isn't for sale. But in exchange for a good piece of trading goods, I and the bolt can help anyone who is oppressed by barrenness. Such is the will of the Guardians. They elect a man—just any man, like me—to help others in this matter."

"What does the bolt look like?" asked Whitespear.

For an answer, Jay opened his bag and pulled out a stone. Never had Whitespear seen anything resembling it. He knew the precious flint, which gave you the finest hunting weapons; the white quartzite, which you could (with some trouble) fashion into good javelin tips; the red sandstone, which could give you your axe but also, by bad luck, a splinter in the eye; the yellow firestone, which he bore in his pouch. This smooth stone, however, with its strange shape was new to him. As he held it in his hand, it looked like the rising male member, softly rounded and noble, tapering into a point. There could be no doubt: this was Guardian work. It was a thing of incredible beauty and perfection. He was deeply moved; the tears came into his eyes. An immense, silent power seemed to pass from the stony member into his fingers.

"You have my promise, Jay," he said. "For the use of this, the finest piece of goods in my pack is yours."

The trader smiled. Kite put out her hand and took the bolt. She bent over it, scrutinizing it closely, passing it between her fingers.

"The way to use it," said Jay solemnly, "is my secret, which I share only with the shamans. And the thing to be done must not be done before your eyes, Whitespear. Still, when it is done, your success is ensured, and within nine moons you shall have a son."

Kite was still bending over the bolt, but Whitespear could glimpse a smile on her lips. "You are right, Jay," she said softly. "The power of the Guardians does indeed live in this bolt, and it will help us."

The trader smiled again and licked his lips. Kite looked up and pushed her hair away from her brow, and at the sight of the shaman symbol Jay flinched as if at a blow. Kite looked at him coldly.

"I am Kite daughter of Harrier, from Swidden Moor. I am a shaman and the daughter of a shaman. How to use the bolt I know best myself, and Whitespear, not you, will assist me. Do not fear; you shall have it back tomorrow, and as for your reward, you can choose among Whitespear's treasures."

The trader's hands were flinging about wildly. He stammered, "I—I didn't know—I ask your forgiveness, Kite—I didn't mean to walk on the ground of the shamans—I want no reward—"

"You have my promise, and I'm not going back on it," said Whitespear. "I want you to have my finest treasure, and so it must be, or the bolt will lose its power."

Jay wiped the sweat from his brow. For once, he was speechless. But out of the darkness came peculiar, half-choked sounds. It was Cuckoo, lying on his face with both hands stuffed into his mouth, heroically trying to stop himself from laughing. Jay cast a furious glance at him.

"Oh, what a woman! T'chk, t'chk, t'chk! What a woman!" groaned Cuckoo.

Kite smiled sweetly at the discomfited trader. "Come, Whitespear," she said. "We'll meet you at sunup, Jay."

They went away into the darkness. Heather, who had been watching with a benevolent air, rose and followed them at a tactful distance, still chewing.

MULLEIN

To the southwest, Veyde's Island rose from the sea in a sheer cliff the height of six men. If, in wintertime, you went out on the sea-ice and looked at the face of the cliff, you would see many shapes and many colors; but if you chose your ground, suddenly you would behold a mammoth and a bison: eternal protectors, never to be dislodged. Above the cliff there rose a pine tree. It had endured many fates and now was weirdly shaped. Originally, it had grown in a north-south fissure of the rock, but an autumn storm many years before had pulled it down. Yet the tree did not die. Some of its roots were still in the ground, although most were clawing the air, and it went on growing. A great branch pointed skyward: it became the new stem of the tree. The old one withered away. And so the tree took tenfold strength: its back to the cliff, its roots in the ground, it spurned all the western storms.

Many years later, a hoodie crow alighted on the top shoot of that pine. She sat down delicately, being a beautiful crow, in all her self-conscious elegance, and as she did so, the top shoot broke beneath her feet. With an affronted scream she flew off, much piqued at being made to feel like a fool, and from that moment, three of the four side-shoots took over and became the new stems of the tree. Thus the pine tree came to form a kind of seat in the place where the stem divided into three parts, a seat where you could sit and look out at the world, shielded from below by the bushy branches.

That pine-tree seat was Mullein's favorite place. It looked out over the next island to the west, which they called Meadow Island, but she could also look south over the sea and north to the mainland beyond the sound. Many times she had been the one to discover game on the mainland shore meadows.

When the sea-ice broke up in the spring, she would sit in the tree and wait for the long-tailed ducks. And in the autumn, she would wait for the storms. They pushed and pulled at the tree; it rocked a little but remained defiantly upright, and she rejoiced in its strength and serenity amid the turbulence of sound, the wailing wind, the crashing waves.

But there was something else, and even more important. Maybe it had to do with her stutter, for here she lost it. She would speak out loud, long monologues in which, for once, she mastered the words: they would forge along as freely as the waves of the sea. She formulated her thoughts in eloquent periods—thoughts that otherwise seemed to stumble over each other, making her speech falter and fall to pieces. Here, too, she would reconstruct those discussions in which her replies had been broken and unintelligible, and substitute clever, profound utterances that won everybody's admiration.

Now it was a day in late summer, misty and heavy with moist heat. Thunderclouds were shouldering up above the mainland. The night before, there had been distant sheet lightning, silent and foreboding, and once a terrific clap of thunder near by, yet the longed-for rain did not come. All the things that grow were dry and rustling after many days of sun, the birches had yellow leaves among the green, the grass was brown, and the orpine was turning red. All the world was as if encapsulated, waiting for the rain.

Suddenly, Mullein saw something new. There was a fire somewhere on Meadow Island; a strand of smoke was curling over the trees. She froze, struck by an idea: the thunderbolt!

Two summers earlier, Kite had been cured of barrenness. She had told Mullein all about it, and they had laughed together at the trader from the South who had attempted to trick Kite. "Still, the bolt was good medicine, and it worked," Kite had said, "and I know already that I'm carrying Whitespear's child. And Jay doesn't bear a grudge: Whitespear gave him his best spear-straightener, and we parted as friends."

"Oh, Kite, if only *you* could have got that bolt!" Mullein exclaimed. "Just think what it would mean to me—to all B-brown women!"

Kite nodded sadly. The bolt was Jay's, and he would never give it away. Indeed, that was right and proper: such a treasure could not be exchanged for anything less than equally precious work of the Guardians. The idea of stealing it did not even occur to them: that would have destroyed its powers.

Nine moons later, when the long-tailed duck in their thousands dotted the sea everywhere, Kite gave birth to a son. He was named Wolf after his father's mother's father. But the Whites called him Sea Kale, and his bird was the sand-piper.

And so Mullein's belief in the powers of the bolt was confirmed. After that, she looked hopefully to the sky when-ever the clouds towered up. But she seemed to be under a spell; she could not remember another summer so free of thunderstorms. Gradually, she forgot all about it.

But now! Lightning had struck somewhere on Meadow Island and something was on fire, perhaps a tree. Then there might be a thunderbolt in the tree, like the one described by Kite, a powerful magic stone that would make the impossi-ble come true, a bolt that could make her, a Brown woman, fertile. If she could find it, she would become a new woman, a real one, one who didn't stutter, one who was held in honor.

One who could help others! Kite knew how to use the magic bolt. Together, they would give all the Brown women a new life.

Her thoughts ran on while she climbed down and hastened towards the ford. Avens can come home, she thought, Gale can come home. She jumped from one hogback to another, slid down a moss-covered incline, and all but ran into a dead pine tree that was in her way, grey and gnarled, its twigs like the extended fingers of an old man. Gusts of wind soughed restlessly in the alders when she stepped into the water. With a great surge of wings a flock of starlings rose overhead, a thickening and thinning cloud of birds, banking sheerly as if governed by a single will. Towards the sea, a couple of har-bor seals slipped noiselessly into the water.

Yes, Avens can give up her plans. Mullein knew much more about them than she had let on to anybody. The mes-sage had reached her, as it had Marten and Gale: *Join us! We need you! It is the day of the Browns!* And Marten and Gale had gone. But Mullein had hesitated, and in the end she had asked Marigold for counsel, though she should have known that she wouldn't get any sense out of her.

"Leave them alone," said Marigold with a laugh. "Why seek death in the wilderness when you can have a good time here? Can you see *me* running around in strange forests?"

She stretched her lazy, gleaming body and cast a derisive glance at her sister. "You do as you like. I have better things to think about. Valerian is going to get a pike for me. I'm teaching him to make love. He's improving, Mullein, he's improving!"

Mullein grinned at the memory while she made her way through the dense alders on the shore of Meadow Island. No, Marigold would never take anything seriously—anything, that is to say, beyond her immediate vision. She was warm-hearted and would go to endless trouble on your behalf—if you were within sight. Anything else was just a tale, to laugh at and forget.

A great gust of wind whipped through the pine-crowns, and there was a sharp crack as a tree-trunk snapped off somewhere. Mullein stopped to listen. There was a crackling of broken branches, then silence: the tree hadn't fallen to the ground but was caught by another tree. Out of the wood came a plaintive noise, a broken tree rubbing against another as it swayed in the wind. A hare came scampering, saw her, and broke away. A flock of clouds careened across the sky; their linings glittered in the sun and then were turned off as if by the hand of a giant. Mullein started to run as fast as she could towards the place where she had seen the pillar of smoke.

. . .

The wind was veering this way and that. There was a sudden hail of sparks. In front of Mullein a pine exploded into flame, all its needles flaring up simultaneously, and she felt the heat against her face. The fire jumped to the next tree. She orbited around the fire, anxiously looking for the place where it had started. Where, where? She couldn't find it. She ran in a dither from tree to tree. Here was a burning birch: the heat drove her back. And then came the storm.

The wind came in an immense slap. Many trees broke, and the burning birch went down in a whirlpool of fire. Mullein was to windward of the fire, she was safe, but she clenched her fists in a rage: there was the fire, there, there, and there. Why was this storm taking everything away from her, hiding the magic thunderbolt? The flames were spreading rapidly eastward.

Something died within her. At the same time, she was struck by a new thought:

I saw the fire! I should have given warning!

Now it was too late. The fire-storm was rushing inexorably upon Veyde's Island. "O Guardians!" she cried, raising her hands, "Stop the fire! Stop it! Save them! Save them, save Veyde's Island, save me!"

On her knees, weeping, she crept towards the fire until it almost singed her face. The Powers had decided: Veyde's Island was to die.

Was there any hope? She leaped up. Maybe the people had had time to save themselves. Mullein ran to the south shore of Meadow Island. Here she was quite safe as long as the wind blew from the west. She came down to a cove that was sheltered from the wind. A large rock stood out in the water. Mullein waded out to it and climbed up to the summit.

Veyde's Island was on fire. It was smothered in smoke, a great black cloud driven along by the storm, yet above it she saw the blinding puffs of fire as one pine tree after another burst into flame. But away to the south was a long, treeless point, and there she saw people moving about. So they, at least, had escaped. Mullein fetched a deep breath.

Standing up, she stretched out her right arm straight to the side and held her left arm obliquely upward: that was her sign. For a long time she remained like that, while the wind tore at her back. Finally she saw one of the distant figures raise both arms, pointing straight up. That was Veyde's sign, and she knew that they had seen her. Shaking with fatigue, she let her arms fall and lay down on the smooth crest of the rock.

.   .   .

When the fire-storm erupted over Veyde's Island, Hind was alone in the summer village. The small group of skin-clad tents was situated on the high ground above the cliff, not far from Mullein's pine tree. If the Whites had been asked why they chose to spend their summers there rather than in the winter houses, they would have answered, "It is the custom," or perhaps simply, "Because it is handy." Actually it was a tradition dating back to their forebears, who were wanderers and followed the game from season to season, as did still their fellow tribesmen in the far North.

Families with small children lived in a group of tents farther east, where the shore was low and shelving. Here, too, the tents were empty because the children and most of their elders had walked out on the long moraine split that thrust into the sea in the south.

Hind was busy with her wine. The bilberry mash had started to ferment. At the last full moon, when the Powers were congenial, she had added a leavened brew of sweet gale and raspberries, and now the wine was tumultuously alive in every skin: its spirit was in power. She would have loved to see Kite there, and looked forward to the evening, when Kite had promised to be back, bringing little Wolf with her. Hind's grandchild! She lost herself in happy dreams. The Powers had not failed her. She had a son, and now he had a son. In them, she and Tiger would live on. She had everything that she could wish for.

Suddenly she smelled the smoke. Frightened, she opened the tent flap and looked out. At that very moment the storm struck, blowing down all the tents. Around her the pines went up in flames, and the fire ran along in the dry grass.

Hind cried out in terror and crawled out of the ruined tent. A rain of sparks blew by, and some caught in her hair. As she struck at them with her hands to kill them, she crawled backward. Suddenly she felt empty air under her feet: she was at the edge of the cliff. She closed her eyes, but the blaze penetrated through her eyelids. She was lying on the outermost crest, her legs dangling over the cliff, the fire raging before her.

Thus she lay an eternity of eternities. Her face was singed, her hair was burned off, her eyes lost their light, and still her fingers clawed into the ground.

When the rain came she did not believe her senses.

. . .

Tiger was on his way to the summer village when the storm broke. Together with Whitespear, Kite, and little Wolf, he had spent a couple of days on the mainland. Now they had sighted bison to the north: Veyde must be told. Whitespear stayed on the mainland to keep an eye on the bison and to look for useful objects on the shore, but Kite and the child came along on the raft with Tiger to Veyde's Island. There mother and child remained on the north shore, where bilberries and raspberries were plentiful, while Tiger loped away through the wood.

Suddenly there was thick smoke streaming through the pine-crowns. Tiger realized that the forest was burning. During all his years on Veyde's Island, he had not experienced a forest fire, but it held no terrors for him, or for the Whites: inland they had witnessed many fires. It was easy to avoid an advancing fire. Animals, struck by terror, would run straight away and get caught; man, who was clever, would run athwart the wind and save himself. Tiger accordingly turned south, and as the smoke became denser and the ominous din of the fire increased, he reached the southern

point of the island. Most of the Whites were there, and
Veyde was among them.

"Tiger!" she said with a broad grin. "Did you get your
beard singed? We are all here, and I saw Mullein on Meadow
Island."

Tiger looked from one to the other. "Where is Hind?"

The color drained from Veyde's cheeks and she was silent.
Tiger gripped her shoulders and shook her. "Veyde! Have
you let her die?" he cried, beside himself.

"I thought that—that she was with you," Veyde faltered.
"But then . . . then maybe she is up in the summer village."

Tiger stepped back. Veyde collapsed, shielding her face
with her hands. She had been at fault, forgetting Hind.

Tiger looked towards the distant cliff. It could be glimpsed
from moment to moment through the stream of smoke. The
storm was ripping up a terrific sea, even in the closed bay,
and the spray from the breakers rained over them. Turning
north, they saw the island burning. Alders and rowans
would burn down, but their roots would live on and grow
new shoots. The pines took the fire in their heads and flared
up in explosion after explosion, yet many of them would
remain alive. But the birches died in a conflagration of unen-
durable heat.

Right at the edge of the cliff, Tiger could see something.
He hesitated, then ran out into the breakers and started to
work north along the shore. Time and again he was thrown
down, but he got up and fought on.

He was halfway there when the rain started.

.   .   .

"Hind, my dearest!"
Her fingers were buried in the moss. Her hair was singed; a
few strands were pasted to her cheeks in the rain. She opened
her eyes.

"My legs," she said. "They've fallen off, I think."

He laughed out of sheer relief. "Oh no, they're here."

"I thought I was blind. But I can see you, Tiger."

He held her in his arms. "It is over, Hind. All is well."

"Whitespear? Wolf? Kite?"

"All safe."

"Is that true?"

Up to that moment, Tiger had thought it was true. Now, suddenly, he was struck by doubt and terror.

"Is it true?"

The rain poured down upon them.

HEATHER

The b i s o n are far away, thought Heather lazily. Then Miss Kite is safe, and the God-child too.

He looked east along the shore. The distance was about two slingshot-lengths, that was just about right: he could keep watch without intruding. There they were—Miss Kite, Mister Whitespear, Mister Tiger. He gave a contented sigh. All is well—and I have a new lump of resin.

The heat was oppressive, and his thoughts began to wander. For a while he thought about his woman, Miss Orache, and their small daughter, Loosestrife, who might—why not? —become the leader of the islanders one day. He blinked at the sun. Over the forest, great clouds were towering up. If only it would rain, thought Heather. Why, I can make it rain, he told himself, I will just go and ask the Guardian! In his dream, he roamed far and wide. But then the sun darkened, and now the Guardian of the mammoth appeared, she who had once brought them to disaster. She carried a horn in her hand. She came closer and closer; he shrank before her commanding eyes; she said, "Drink!" He tried to defend himself, but his hands were powerless. The giant horn arched up in front of him.

Heather awoke with a start. The sky was clouding over, and fitful blasts of wind were tearing at the withered grass. He looked east. They were gone! No, there was a crouching figure among the boulders. It looked like Mister Whitespear. Where was Miss Kite?

He looked south across the sound to Veyde's Island, and was relieved to see the raft approaching the other shore. His goddess was going home. It was time for him to follow.

He went down to the water's edge, where he had pulled up his coracle. During his two summers on Veyde's Island he had learned to handle the craft almost as well as the islanders. The boat was made of thin rods covered with skin, and the paddle consisted of a flat piece of wood lashed to a handle.

He pushed the boat out and started to paddle across the smooth surface.

The first gust of wind came quite unexpectedly and almost caused the boat to capsize. Heather gave a surprised grunt. With an angry hiss the water came to life: innumerable small waves lapped at the sides of the coracle. He looked west, right into the wind, and caught sight of a foaming white line that was rushing at him with incredible speed. He had little experience of hard weather at sea, and it was from pure instinct that he made the only right move and turned the prow to the wind. When the storm-wave reached him, the coracle rode over it. The wave was followed by another and yet another, and soon he was surrounded by boiling seas and whipping spray. Grunting with dismay now, he toiled to keep the coracle turned into the wind, for he was convinced that it would turn turtle at once if he let it go.

He looked again at the island and was met by a sight that made him freeze with terror.

An immense cloud of smoke was rolling in from the west and engulfing Veyde's Island at fantastic speed. It surged forth at treetop level, and above the cloud the flames rose and fell like evil blossoms swiftly burgeoning and withering. The sky was covered with low, scudding clouds, red-tinged by the reflection of the blaze. While Heather still sat thunderstruck, a great wave pushed the coracle to one side and all but turned it over. He made a few rapid strokes with his paddle. Although he was now paddling against the wind for all he was worth, the coracle was carried eastward by the wind and the waves. He tried to work sideways towards Veyde's Island, which was now a single gigantic furnace. He did get a little closer, but it was slow work, and all the time he was slipping farther east.

The waves were growing ever bigger. He was surrounded by flying spray, and the shore was all but invisible. All he could do now was to try and keep afloat, to endure. But the water was up to his hips already and the coracle moved sluggishly, while water poured into it. A great wave broke over the prow, over the boat, over Heather's head.

. . .

Whitespear had always been keenly interested in the things that were to be found on the shore. He had been prowling around, collecting driftwood and stones in a heap; now he sat down to investigate them. He was quite aware that Heather had followed them to the mainland. He found the patient attention of the White man amusing as well as touching, although irritating at times.

After an interested glance at Whitespear's collection, Tiger went off with Kite and Wolf to raise a hunting party on the island. From where he was, Whitespear could observe the bison far away on the shore meadows to the northeast. They had not moved. Whitespear returned to his contemplation of a peculiar dark-brown stone. It was banded in lighter and darker colors and tended to split into thin, flat shivers. He liked to hold the stone in his hand and feel its parts separating, revealing the pink, grainy interior, so unlike the smoothly patinated surface.

The stones gave him great pleasure. Yet stonework was not his strong point; Avens was better at that. He remembered how she would look at the hand-axes that she had struck, tenderness showing in her eyes. In the same way he looked at these sea-smoothed stones, all different to the eye, all with a feel of intimacy, a comfortable weight in his hand. So many shapes, so many colors. The spirits of the rocks were good: they wanted to serve. They are in league with us, Whitespear thought, there is no guile in them. The great Powers have no honor, but these, the simplest and lowliest —the spirits of the trees, the rocks, the grass—they can be trusted.

Avens! Such a long time since she had been in his thoughts. He looked up as if expecting to see her, and just then the first fierce gust of wind sent a blinding shower of sand into his eyes. Swearing, he tottered down to the water to wash his eyes. While he was still at it, he felt the wind increasing and heard a mysterious humming that grew louder. When the storm came, he was knocked down.

It took him a while to get the sand out of his eyes. When he was at last able to see, Veyde's Island was already in flames.

Of all those who saw that sight, none was ever to forget it, but among them all, Whitespear was struck by the greatest terror and anguish. A little while ago he had seen his woman, his son, and his father headed that way, and now the whole island was turning into a great pyre. He uttered a cry, which was torn from his lips by the wind so that it was inaudible even to himself, and ran along the shore. He had to get there, he had to save them.

The raft was gone. Whitespear remembered that Heather had a coracle. He looked to the west, where he had seen Kite's White slave, but he was gone too. His gaze flitted over the raging water—yes, there was a boat. It must be Heather. Would he make it? There were glimpses of the coracle through the flying spray and foaming waves, then it was gone.

Realizing that he was left without a boat, Whitespear raised his fists and cursed the Powers. But he regained his senses and his memory. He had seen a stranded log someplace. It was impossible to swim across the sound, but with the help of a log . . .

He ran on. There it was—a driftwood log with all its branches snapped off, a long-dead tree-trunk thrown up on the shore. Holding on to the log, Whitespear pushed it out into the water. Then, resting one arm on it, he started to swim.

After only a few strokes, he realized that he would never make it. Still he fought on. The waves, their crests flattened by the pressure of the wind, struck at him incessantly like the open palm of an enemy, and the unremitting blows soon drove everything out of his brain except the will to endure, to survive, to get there. Meanwhile, the waves carried him ever farther to the east, away from Veyde's Island, and he clung to the log, forgetting everything else. The rain came down, the waves and the wind moderated a little, and he drifted on without thinking, feeling, or caring.

He felt bottom under his feet. It was a shore. To his eyes it seemed utterly foreign, as if he was entering an unknown world. He crawled ashore and slumped down.

· · ·

Wolf, Kite's son, was fifteen moons old—not that she had kept count. At about the time of the summer solstice he had learned to walk. Now he would toddle off proudly, toes pointing inward, and fall over stones and tree-roots, but get up on his own. He was a cheerful child and never cried for long, but smiled all the more and talked a great deal. What he was actually saying almost nobody knew, but Kite sometimes caught a word or two. The word he was now repeating with great satisfaction signified "bilberries." He was sitting by a bilberry plant covered with fruit, and he was utterly happy. As if deep in thought, he picked the berries one by one and put them in his mouth.

Kite, squatting beside him, looked at him smilingly and sometimes gave him a helping hand. She was captivated by his methodical earnestness and unconsciously mimicked his movements with her own hands. He had been the center of her life since his birth, even since she knew that she was with child. She had forgotten all her ambitions, all her religious brooding, all her anxiety about Whitespear and his obstinacy. She lived in the present, happy at each new day, at the boy's first smile, at his prattling in which she proudly distinguished real words, at his first tooth, at his first courageous steps.

He would become a great man. Yes, in him the heritage from Harrier and Whitespear was united: the wisdom of the shaman, the skill of the artist. A hero to men and women in the summers of the future, honored and sung among Blacks and Whites. What else, with such an ancestry? And Hind, who loved him as much as Kite, agreed passionately.

The trees stirred in the first gusts of the storm. Kite at once lifted up the boy, who cried out angrily when torn away from the berries. Kite pulled up a bilberry plant to have something to pacify him. It was going to be a real storm, and she had to find open ground to keep away from falling trees. She went down to the shore, where a big flat rock jutted into the water. That was where Tiger had pulled up the raft. They would be safe here, for the only trees near by were small alders. Kite put the boy on the ground and held out the berries to him: "Come, eat!" Contentedly, Wolf started to pick them.

Kite now caught the reek of smoke. A forest fire, she told herself. She was not alarmed: she knew about forest fires. The wind was coming from the west, and so you should go north or south. Well, she had gone north, and here she was at the north shore. In front of her was the water. I have never seen water burn, Kite told herself with a smile, and in any case I have a raft here! Yes, if the worst came to the worst she could take off with the raft and paddle across to the mainland.

But when she looked at the sound she became uneasy, for it did not look familiar at all. A little while ago it had been smooth and glassy; now great waves were tossing out there. Kite was no sailor, but she remembered crossing the sound with Whitespear once in a westerly gale. "Tie yourself to the raft if it blows hard," he had told her. "The logs are slippery and you could get washed into the sea." So he had tied a strap around her waist and fastened it to the raft. And she, who always sought new knowledge, had asked him how he did it, and he had taught her how to make the knots. She knew.

The smoke was denser, and there were glimpses of fire in the distance. She would have to act. She had a long strap handy, the one she used for a carryall slung across her shoulder. Now she fastened the strap around Wolf, put him on the raft, and secured the strap to one of the thongs that held the logs together. For herself she had nothing, but if things got bad, she told herself, she could put her arm through the thong.

There was a shower of sparks. The fire was here; it glowed in her face and sent sparks raining through the air. She pushed the raft into the water, jumped aboard, and took the paddle.

They drifted out. For a moment they were in smooth

water; then came the first waves, and the fury of their assault made it clear to Kite that the paddle would be useless. She lay down beside Wolf, threaded her right arm under one of the thongs, and put her left arm around the child.

There was no going back. The shore was already an inferno.

· · ·

Old people said that it was such a storm as came about only once in a lifetime. The island people knew the autumn storms, which were greatly feared not only because of their violence but also because of the darkness and cold with which they were associated. But in the summer! It could happen that the Guardians of the sea and the winds let off a tempest of unthinkable fury and suddenness. Then it sometimes struck from two directions, first one and then the other, while in between the skies cleared and a deathly silence descended over the heaving sea with its restlessly pulsing swell. At such times it was hard to know what to do. The Guardians of the east and west winds had fallen out and were at spears drawn, roaring in inexplicable enmity, forgetting the earthly beings who were dependent on them. And so it was this time.

To those who were ashore it did not mean so much. Broken trees marked the path of the storm, and bison and elk found new and unexpected forage. But to those who were at sea it became a revelation of evil, an experience of ultimate terror. And so it was for Kite.

Years afterwards it would return in her dreams. Or even when she was awake: then she shied, put her hand before her eyes, whimpered, tried to think of something else, think as hard as she could, and yet her blood would run cold and she would be back out there with her arm around her child, the small child who still could cry, who lived through it all, half smothered like herself, the child whom she loved more than life itself.

In her dreams it was still worse.

The raging seas became an enemy that was lashing out at her and her child as the Powers strove to drown them. Inexorably, with a living hatred, they seemed to be regaling themselves with her pain. And yet there was a respite, a moment for breathing, when Kite would hear the child's cries: yes, the cruel play was continuing. All these summers and winters the sea had deceived her with its dissembling goodwill. Now its great spirit was standing upright, he was laughing, stalking her and her child.

Then—the assault. The giant had chosen his victims. A breath ago I was only amusing myself. Now I'll get you.

The crash, the terrifying splintering sound when the great wave-trough laid the very sea-bottom bare and the stricken raft fell to pieces.

A pale face in front of her, a firm grip around her waist. It was Heather.

Afterwards he told her, in his timid way, of how his boat foundered beneath him, how he rode the waves, how he saw the raft close by and was able to reach it.

The superhuman strength of the White man saved them. He carried them both ashore in his arms, put them tenderly on the ground and stood up, smiling triumphantly. He had delivered his goddess, he had saved the God-child. Then he too collapsed, pressing his hands to his chest.

.   .   .

Kite never went back to Veyde's Island. As soon as she could stand on her legs, she turned her back to the sea. The Powers had given her a lesson, and she had understood.

Too long, said the Powers, too long have you lived with one who defies us; too long have you lived without Shelk in your heart. Yet you learned from your father to search for Shelk's will and to obey it. Now we have shown you Shelk's will, but in our clemency we have let the White man rescue you.

You shall depart and leave your old life. You shall search for wisdom, and that you will find among the shamans and the White healers. You shall take your son and bring him up to be a shaman in the faith of Shelk. But with the father of that son you shall have nothing to do, until he recants.

Thus Kite started on her journey with her small son and her White slave, for wherever she went Heather would also go. She realized that that, too, was in accordance with the Powers' will and that it had been meant from the outset: when she gave Heather his life, and when he saved her and her child from certain death. Shelk had ordained it: she had a compact with Heather. Now Heather had been elected to help and protect her and the child during the journey. Alone, they would surely have perished.

Where she would go and what was to happen, that she knew not, but she was sure it would be revealed when the time came.

"I wish to find Mister Helleborine," she said.

"I know where to find him," Heather answered.

V E Y D E

A t a l l B r o w n man walked silently through the devastated landscape. He carried a light pack, and out of his quiver the shafts of several spears rose above his head. He looked around, his face wooden, showing neither surprise nor sorrow. Many of the pines, though little more than scorched skeletons, were still standing, but the ground was covered with half-burned logs. He scratched desultorily in the ashes with his toes. Here the fire cranesbill would grow, the raspberry would build thorny thickets, the rosebay would flower like a pool of flame. All the fire's children among grasses and herbs would have their time. Then birches would grow up. A generation later, the forest would be back.

He was looking for a woman, and he found her on the southern point. Here the wood was untouched by flames:

the fire had passed by to the north and had been put out by the rain before it had time to spread.

She was sitting on a log, suckling her child. She looked up wonderingly and passed her hand over her eyes in greeting. Her gaze was sad and inquiring.

"Miss Orache," said the man, "I have a message to you from Mister Heather."

"Then he is alive," she said with a smile. "I am grateful to you for those words, Mister Marten."

"Do not search for him," said Marten. "He will let you know when the time comes."

"I will wait."

"But not here. Go to Blue Lake: the village is empty and the country is good. I shall see to it that you have safe-conduct: that will be my task now. Here"—and Marten looked around at the wasteland—"here you cannot stay."

"I will tell them. They have moved to Meadow Island. But I stayed here, waiting—"

Marten cast a thoughtful glance at Meadow Island, green and fair in the distance. "You cannot live there. There is no spring on Meadow Island."

"No," Orache agreed with a sigh, "the only spring is here on Veyde's Island, and there is a curse on it now."

"Go to them and tell them what I have said."

"Are you not coming too, Mister Marten?"

"I should like to, but I cannot. I was bringing other messages, tidings for Miss Mullein and Miss Marigold, but all is changed now. I have promised you safe-conduct and I must act. The safe-conduct holds for my father Tiger and my brother Whitespear too, but only to the land around Blue Lake. They must not go north. Tell them that!"

He left without waiting for an answer.

. . .

The warning came too late.

Whitespear found the tracks of the fugitives on the shore. He could not mistake Kite's footprints: no other woman on Veyde's Island had such a small foot. There, too, little Wolf had toddled along on his own for a bit. The big feet were of course Heather's. So they were alive, they had escaped the fire and the storm. But they were going away, inland. Where? Why?

It was good to know that Heather was with them, that they had not struck out alone. But where was Kite going and what was she looking for? That she was the one who had made the decision he did not doubt. Heather would obey her and he would never desert her.

She had often talked about Helleborine, the great White healer. Could she be looking for him? Or might she be on her way back home to Swidden Moor, to her father Harrier, Otter's willful shaman?

He ran along in their tracks, and so it came about that he did not notice Marten's unmistakable footprints. He did not even observe that they had met and spoken to each other, although the encounter was clearly written in tracks on the clayey ground. He lost the track and found it again. An old, well-trodden path led towards the cloudberry moors of the Whites, far inland, the place they called Miss Sundew's Cloudberries. He ran on without rediscovering the tracks: the path was covered with pine-needles and kept its secret.

Two days had passed since the storm. For two days he had searched in vain, without a thought of food, without seeing anybody, at first along the water's edge, then over the patches of soft ground that would take prints.

The sun was low in the western sky when he came up on a long, winding esker. Here the pines grew sparsely, and the path followed the crest. As he ran on, the sunshine struck him in regular flashes between the pine-trunks, in a rapid rhythm that seemed to hammer at his brow and burn into his brain. Everything else seemed to vanish; there remained only the fierce, stabbing light, flash–flash–flash. His head was swimming, and suddenly he crashed to the ground.

That night he slept as he had fallen. In the morning he awoke with a clear head. Now he saw his way. First of all he had to hunt, to get food. Then he could plan his journey.

He would go to Blue Lake and its abandoned village. From there he would go on into the unknown north country, the land of the Whites. If they had gone that way, he would find their tracks easily enough. Kite would seek out the White villages and ask for news of Helleborine.

If they had not gone that way, well, then they must be going to Swidden Moor. And he would change direction and go south, or southwest.

Whitespear rose, feeling invigorated. He had made his decision. They were alive, and he would find them, wherever they were.

·   ·   ·

Whitespear had been so busy searching that he did not notice a coracle that set out from Veyde's Island and started across the sound. There were three people in the boat, which was the largest of the two coracles on the island and the only one left after Heather's shipwreck.

Hind, who had long been unconscious after her tribulations, was desperate. She wanted to leave right away to search for Whitespear and Kite. Veyde had set the small, dejected group of Whites on Meadow Island to work building a raft. However, one of them, Miss Rosebay, suddenly remembered that she had used the big coracle the day before the fire and that she had pulled it up on the northwest shore of Veyde's Island, in a place where it might have escaped destruction. As it turned out, she was right. The boat was safe and sound, except for some burns on the gunwale.

Tiger and Hind made ready to set out.

"I am coming with you," said Veyde.

"You are needed here," Tiger objected.

Veyde, however, declined to stay behind. Miss Rosebay could take over for her. Actually, she was deeply troubled by the thought that she had done nothing to succor Hind during the fire. Maybe she could make amends this way.

After the storm, the weather was chilly but clear, with a whiff of autumn in the air. As soon as they passed the northwest point of the island, they spotted Whitespear on the opposite shore. They called out and waved to him, but he did not see them and their voices did not carry through the north wind. They saw him vanish into the woods.

The footprints told their story. "They were here, so they are alive," Tiger said. "Look, these are Wolf's tracks. He ran across the sand, then Heather picked him up. Afterwards, they walked into the forest."

"They've gone away!" cried Hind, desolated.

"And Whitespear went the same way. Oh, look! Marten was here. He went down to the shore."

"Then he must be on the island," said Veyde hopefully. "Maybe he knows something about them." And she looked towards the island that bore her name, as if expecting to see her son on the shore.

Tiger, who had been searching the ground, shook his head. "Here are his tracks again. He came back the same way. And he was running!"

They were silent for a while, distilling the sequence of events in their minds. It ran like this: Here, Marten came across Kite and Heather. He went down to the shore, but Kite and Heather went into the wood. Then Marten returned, running at full tilt. Much later, Whitespear appeared and went into the wood.

What could it all mean? Hind embraced Tiger eagerly. "My boy! And the little one! Tiger, you must bring them back. Back to me!"

"But where did they go?" asked Tiger. "I'm going to lose the track."

Veyde understood enough of the Black tongue to know what they were saying. "Miss Kite often talked about Mister Helleborine," she ventured.

"So she did," said Tiger. "But where is he? Not at Blue Lake. There is nobody there at all."

"He is at Caribou Lake," said Veyde. "Gale told me. Yes, she came here once, in secret."

On hearing this, Tiger decided to leave for Caribou Lake right away. No, said Veyde, he must not go alone, she would go with him. They argued about this for a while, but Veyde was adamant. Just what Gale had told her she would not say, but she would come along, and the best thing would be for Tiger to stay at home. Hind, who did not understand what they were saying, burst into tears, and when Tiger translated for her, she repeated that he must go, for she did not trust Veyde. Tiger, although he wanted to go, thought this preposterous, and there was another scene. They stamped about on the shore, waving their arms and shouting at each other.

In the end it was decided that Tiger and Veyde would go to Caribou Lake, Hind would return to Meadow Island, and Rosebay would become the leader of the Whites in Veyde's absence.

.   .   .

Three moon-quarters later, Veyde and Tiger reached the end of their journey. Their destination had been Caribou Lake, and they had old marks to lead them there, for they had made the journey once before, long ago. They often talked about the Land of the Osprey, which was the Whites' name for the country around Caribou Lake. Many winters ago they had been there, witnessing the power of Shelk in his lifetime and his final demise.

So far they had gone unnoticed. The Brown protectors of the land, going singly or in pairs, ranged far and wide. They were Avens's warriors and they were singleminded in their dedication.

No Black man is permitted in the land of the Whites. Send them off, kill them if need be: such is the will of Shelk, Shelk the Destroyer, the Evening Star, he of the stern countenance, he who carries the spear and axe of the Avenger. The Blacks may be good or evil before man; here in the northern land they are all the tools of the evil Powers. Keep the Black pestilence away from the land of the Whites: such was the task of the Browns, the living dead.

And the worst interloper is the Black man who arrives together with a White woman. On him is the curse of Shelk, and he must die.

Long ago, Tiger and Veyde had been reconciled with Shelk. But that was Shelk the Healer, he who was now the Morning Star. Not the other Shelk.

Birch and aspen turned yellow early this year. In many places there were long stretches of burned forest, sometimes extending side by side with narrow strips of undamaged trees in between. It was the time of the lingonberry, of the calling of rutting elks, of lakes shining in the morning mist, of thrushes in myriad flocks. The drumming of a woodpecker, the chattering of a squirrel, the mad laugh of a distant pack of hyenas like demons in a quarrel. Otherwise silence, silence, silence, soft footfalls on the moss, the rustling of lingonberry brush. Slowly the days shortened, the darkness of winter crept closer. In the burned-off glades, there was a foam of late-flowering mayweed.

They lived off the land through which they traveled, from seeds, berries, and mushrooms to snared woodfowl and hare. Once an elk calf killed by a bear gave them a great meal. There they lingered, and took the bear when it returned.

The old landmarks raised innumerable memories, and they

often spoke of all the things that their life's journey had given them. The early darkness surprised them with their strength unspent, and they were young once more, in a timeless ecstasy of love.

A dipper sat on a rock in the rapids, small and round, a black-and-white ball. Suddenly it became long and narrow, walked in a thoughtful manner into the water, and vanished beneath the foaming surface. Veyde laughed. In a rock fissure, violets were flowering; they were blue like the summer. Tiger picked two: "They are your eyes." Tiger and Veyde lay down, and she rode him with the ease of a young girl and the passion of a woman.

It is the indigo of the woad, the supreme blueness, the one I extract from the green herb, thought Tiger.

They leaped to their feet: one of the Brown protectors had come upon them, as unexpectedly to himself as to them. He saw and understood, gave a low cry, fumbled for his javelin, and threw it at Tiger. But Veyde, too, had seen and understood, and pitched herself in its way: she took it in her chest. By then Tiger had his atlatl ready, and for the first and only time in his life he turned his weapon against a human being.

It hit the Brown man right in the nose, and the point buried itself in the nasal cavity. The man gripped the shaft with both hands and tried to pull it out. A stream of blood rushed from his mouth. He came tottering towards them, wrenched the point out of his face with a last effort, fell prone, and died, choked by his own blood.

.   .   .

Veyde ripped the spear out of her body and sank to the ground. She rolled from side to side, wild with agony and fury.

"Fool that I am!" she screamed. "Fool! Why did I do it? Why did I not let him kill you?"

Tiger pulled up a chunk of moss and pressed it into the wound in an attempt to stop the flow of blood. "Where are you, Kite? Where are you, Helleborine?" he cried madly. He hardly knew what he was saying. Veyde hunched herself in a cramp, a runnel of blood trickled from her mouth.

"All I did was wrong!" she cried. "Why, oh why did I find you, Tiger? Why did I not let you die that time, so many winters ago? I was like the squirrel who takes his marks from the clouds when he buries his seeds for the winter—so did I take my marks from the clouds when I took you for my man. I was out of my senses, I did wrong. The clouds fly where the Guardians bid them and never do they come back. I have no marks left.

"Better had it been for me never to have seen you. Better for you to take the Black woman and flee away from us, home to your own people!"

"Your life has not been in vain," said Tiger. "You have been a good leader to the islanders, to all of us."

Veyde was lying on her side; he thought it eased her a little. He was still pressing the blood-drenched moss into the wound, and he looked about, hoping to find something better—plantain, blood cranesbill. She was silent. He did not know if she had heard his words.

Now she spoke once more, with difficulty, in a low voice: "It is we who die, we, the Whites. You Blacks live on. You take everything away from us, and last of all, our lives. We thought you Gods—oh, we are nothing but fools. The children you give us are living dead, no life quickens in them."

Tiger bent his head without a word.

"Everything passes out of our hands. Everything goes to you, to the Blacks. Yes, the Powers struck us with madness, they made us soft and yielding when we should have been strong. To us you were Gods and children at the same time. Maybe that is what you are, maybe you are younger than we, maybe you are the kind that the Powers love."

For a long time she lay silent. Then she said:

"Now comes Death. Remember me, Tiger, when the long-tailed duck are singing in the spring!"

When she had uttered this, her agony suddenly was gone. She felt a surge of tremendous happiness. She believed herself to be speaking words of love and consolation; she raised her hand as if to give a sign. And before her arose a mysterious picture from her childhood.

It is a still summer evening with calm waters in a shallow cove. Not a puff of wind stirs in the trees, yet ripples are flying over the surface. She knows that it is a school of small fish, nothing more, and yet the picture becomes a vision of something immeasurably important, of a reconciliation and certainty beyond words. The picture is bathed in light and now it drowns in light, she feels an immense joy, she strives towards the light.

Now she reaches it.

·   ·   ·

Tiger stayed on, cradling Veyde's head in his lap. He looked wonderingly at her face, serene in its repose. The dusk was gathering slowly. He could still see the Brown man a few steps away, and the grotesquely destroyed face was an accusation.

He remained there without moving through the night. Many images came to him as the night wore on. He felt rather than thought that his life, too, had come to an end. There was nothing left to draw him away from the place where Veyde had died.

Yet there was one thing he had to do. At daybreak, he took out the great tiger tooth he had inherited from his father.

He had always wanted Marten, his firstborn, the great hunter, to have it. Now he knew that he would turn away from his children with Veyde, the radiant Brown children of whom they had been so proud. They were dead to him, as dead as Veyde herself.

The tooth was to go to Whitespear.

He did not hear the silent footsteps. He never knew of the axe that smashed in his head, killing him instantly. It was wielded by an expert.

SINGLETUSK

Un s e e n b y the protectors, Whitespear entered the northern land. As soon as he had passed the abandoned village of Blue Lake, he had no landmarks; this was unknown country. Born and bred on the coast, he was oppressed in the forest by the feeling that he was in an alien world. In his earlier journeys on the mainland he had always had landmarks, or been in company. Now he had nothing. Often he had a feeling he was not getting anywhere at all. He marched on, the scenery changed around him, and yet he felt that he was tramping on the same spot all the time.

Once he nearly broke down. It was a night of scudding clouds and a thin sliver of moon. The wind, drawing breath and expelling it in resonant gusts, seemed to make solemn pronouncement of a rising flood of darkness. Unfelt and

unseen, the black flood seemed to rise in the murk around
him, and he stopped in a moment of panic, half expecting to
be engulfed by icy water. Senseless words were echoing
within him, words heard long ago, spoken in a strong, clat-
tering voice: Centaury is calling for her mother, the fox is
out of its hole, Centaury is calling for her MOTHER, the SKY is
falling down, the fox is out of its HOLE. Then, in old Silverbirch's voice, almost inaudibly: The water is rising, THE
WATER IS RISING. He started forward, he was running, his
own breath seemed to whisper, whisper, then shriek: Your
spear is broken, your SPEAR is broken, your spear IS broken.
Images of things seen and forgotten, images of things seen
and remembered: a green pike wriggling its firm body in his
hands, Centaury's eyes looking past him, the one-tusked
mammoth rearing up on its hind legs. He was a child and
the rattling voice told him, Centaury is not coming back,
Centaury is NOT coming back. He stumbled and fell, and the
cool, moist moss met his face.

When he got up he glimpsed a light between the tree-
trunks. He went towards it. It was a log fire, a village, kind
White people. He was back in the world of men.

·   ·   ·

They knew nothing of Helleborine or of Kite and Wolf. But
they wanted to help him. They took good care of him, and
more than one woman timidly asked him to give her a child
of the Gods. Such things were far from his thoughts, but he
was beholden to them for their charity, and he did his best.
In return they gave him a girl to guide him to the next
village. She glowed with pride and joy and straddled him
each morning and evening. And so he roved from village to
village in the north country, while the autumn closed in. The
trees shed their leaves. One day the first snowflakes whirled
in the air. Then he knew that the time had come: he must
seek Kite elsewhere. He would go to Swidden Moor.

It was then that he encountered Singletusk for the third time.

The snow had fallen, dense and muffling. It reached up to his calves. The trees were mantled in wet snow, which fell to the ground in big chunks with a muted sound as if from a whisper of its Guardian. The first thing he saw was the giant spoor, and its size sent a tingling down his back. Could it be . . .? Loping along at a steady trot, he followed the tracks. A thought struck him, and he smiled. Here was one thing in which he was superior to the Whites: they could run like the wind for a short stretch, but over long distances they tired easily and had to stop to get their breath. Whitespear, like all the Blacks, was built for endurance. Now he had an additional advantage: he need not stop to hunt for the day, for the generous Whites had provided him with plenty of food in gratitude for his services. He would be able to track the mammoth for two moon-quarters or more.

By midday he sighted the mammoth and knew he was right. It was Singletusk himself. Their compact held. His partner had come to his aid in his time of need, and White-spear turned to the Guardian of the Black Hill with words of thanksgiving. Now he could trust the Powers to lead him to his goal.

·   ·   ·

Many days later, Whitespear came across one of the Brown protectors. He was still following the mammoth, who went first to the southwest, then southward.

The Brown man had been hiding behind a boulder. Now he rose to his full height, the biggest man Whitespear had ever seen. His broad-shouldered body, swathed in thick bearskin, seemed larger than life. He had a great bony face framed by wild locks of hair, his eyes glowered beneath heavy brows, and there was a cruel look about his mouth.

Whitespear, who felt he had never seen a more terrifying creature, stopped in his tracks. This giant could have pulled off his arms and legs with ease.

The monster roared at him to stop—but as he did it in the White language, the order took the form of a polite injunction to stand still, if he would be so kind. The contrast between the words and the tone of voice left Whitespear confused. The giant strode towards him; he carried a mighty spear and a great hand-axe. Whitespear heard him say, "Yes, he has stopped. Why, he is Black, yes, so he is. Then he must die. We have to kill the Blacks who come from the south. But this one comes from the north and is going south. That is odd. I wonder what his name is. What is your name, young man?"

Whitespear stammered his name, and the man repeated it at once. "Whitespear, he is called. Well, well. Funny name. He can speak. He understands what you say to him."

"May you soar high, sir," said Whitespear anxiously. That was the usual greeting of the Whites.

"He is polite, too," observed the Brown giant. "Knows how to behave. Now I ought to be polite myself, and tell him my name. Are you polite to somebody you mean to kill? And is it proper to tell him my name? He can use that in the world of the spirits, if he wants to put a curse on me. My name is Bulrush," said the man and made a sly face. "Now he does not know if it is my right name. Ha! May you soar high," he added.

Whitespear tried frantically to think of some way to appease this terrible foe. "I was just going to eat," he said. "Would you like to share my meal, Mister Bulrush?"

"He thinks I am hungry. He thinks that I will not kill him if I eat his food. He is mistaken. But I do not have to kill him right now. Maybe I should not kill him at all. He is going the wrong way. He is going south. I have to think about it. Thank you, Mister Whitespear, I will accept a morsel of food."

Whitespear was getting used to the man's habit of thinking out loud. Moreover, he had begun to suspect that Bulrush was not as dangerous as he looked. While Whitespear was getting his provisions—dried meat—out of his pack, Bulrush pensively continued:

"He cannot escape me. I can run faster than he and I am much stronger. Anyway, I should like to eat. I can run faster than you," he announced in the roaring voice he adopted when speaking to Whitespear. "I can kill you whenever I like. Do not try to run away, young man."

"Certainly not," Whitespear assured him. "I am searching for my woman—she is Black," he added quickly. "Miss Kite is her name. She is a healer. She is traveling with a White man called Heather."

"He is looking for a Black woman—*here*! It sounds like a lie. But he is so odd that it may be true. Odd names, too— Whitespear, Kite. I think that he is mad. It might be better to kill him right away. Thank you, Mister Whitespear. It tastes excellent. Elk meat, I perceive."

"Miss Kite is looking for a White healer called Helleborine," Whitespear went on. "Do you know him, Mister Bulrush?"

"Mister Helleborine, our healer at Caribou Lake," said Bulrush. "Then maybe he is not mad after all. I had better take him with me. *She* must decide. You had better come with me, Mister Whitespear," roared Bulrush solemnly.

Whitespear conveyed that he would be delighted to do so, and Bulrush gave a dubious grunt. "That remains to be seen. If I know her right, the pleasure will be a short one. I go now. He had better walk in front of me—then he will not do anything silly. I go now," he repeated, turning to Whitespear, "and you can go in front of me. That way."

Bulrush went on talking as they walked. Whitespear thought that probably he had spent much of his life in solitude. Lone walkers often got the habit of talking to themselves—in fact, he had caught himself doing so. Now he listened with great interest and gradually came to understand what was going on.

The Browns had a task: to keep Black men from entering the land of the Whites. Their orders were to stop any intruder that came from the south, if it was a man—women apparently were free to move about. The fact that Whitespear had arrived from the north and was going south had come as a surprise to Bulrush, and he was agonizing out loud about what should be done in such an unprecedented case.

They struck a path and soon met two Browns, a woman and a man. They were fantastically attired in birdskin dresses and festooned with colorful feathers from head to toe. "There are the fops," said Bulrush. "Honest bearskin is good enough for me. May you soar high, Miss Vetch. I have a prisoner here. He can give us important news."

The Browns advanced in a solemn two-person procession, the woman leading. They returned the greeting, but ignored Whitespear. Bulrush went on muttering sarcastic comments long after they had vanished.

They now skirted a remarkable stockade, which appeared to be very old. The logs were grey and rotten and many of them had fallen down. Bulrush, who had become more and more communicative, turned directly to Whitespear with his information: "This is what remains of Shelk's palisade. I myself was born here, by Caribou Lake, in Shelk's own time. My father was one of his warriors. But he is gone and I do not remember him. I grew up in the north country."

Whitespear pondered upon the ruins. Baywillow and Hind had told him the story of how the earthly power of Shelk was broken, right here at Caribou Lake, long ago. And indeed, he could hear the distant thunder of the waterfall that had taken Shelk's body and given it back to Harrier.

Yes, the stockade bore mute evidence. And yet, Whitespear reflected, Shelk's power was not broken: he was greater now than he had been in life. His power lived in men's minds.

Two old pine trees formed a gate in the palisade. There on a fallen log sat a woman with the palm of a caribou antler in her hand and an engraving tool in the other. At the sight of them, she rose. It was Avens.

.   .   .

"Whitespear, you went out to seek Shelk the Healer. Did you find him?"

"Yes, Avens, I did. Only too late."

"No. It wasn't too late, it was in its proper time. What happens is what is meant to happen."

The night had closed in, and they were sitting by a big fire. The flames rose straight up in the still air, and above them hung the stars of autumn. The firelight flickered over a group of people: Avens's Brown protectors. Whitespear glimpsed the fire reflected in a pair of eyes, a hand clutching a wineskin, a figure rising to put more fuel on the blaze. The talk of the Browns blended in a subdued hum with the ceaseless surge of the great waterfall, which would fall silent only when it froze over. One of the Browns suddenly burst into drunken song, a song of wine and fire and death, of spear and blade and club. It was an evil song, and the others drew away from him.

"They are all crazy, each in his own way," said Avens curtly. "That one is a drunkard. Another one thinks he is the son of Shelk. But they are my people and they obey me."

The song ended with a singular image. The Black man lay dead, clubbed and speared. Then Shelk's hand came from on high and gathered him up like a father with his son. Avens turned to Whitespear. "I knew you had found what you sought. I know most things. The Browns are my eyes and ears. You went out and so did I, but for a different reason. I went to seek Shelk the Destroyer."

"Did you find him, Avens?"

"Yes, I found him."

For a moment her face was tired, spent. Then she resumed:

"Do you remember the two dragonflies, Whitespear? One of them killed the other. That was the first sign. When I went out into the world, I found two elks. One of them had palmate antlers, the other had antlers with long points like a stag. They fought, and the stag-elk killed the other. That was the second sign: the Evening Star vanquished the Morning Star. Then I found an old man who lived by himself, with nothing left but his memories: he had been one of Shelk's warriors. From him I learned everything about man-hunting, about discipline and leadership. And by way of thanks I gave him an easy death: he burst his heart when I rode him.

"Then I found the shaman, Shelk's disciple, he who knows how to find out the will of the Powers. You know him, Whitespear: his name is Harrier. A vain man, one who vaunts his powers, but also a kind man and one of great knowledge. I learned all that he knew, and by way of thanks I gave him his life: I straddled him but let him live.

"The third sign was given to me when the days became short that autumn. I met two mammoths, and one of them was Singletusk. They fought, and Singletusk killed the other. Then I made a compact with him, and that compact still holds.

"Yet I had not learned enough, and I became arrogant. I wished to use the Whites for their own good. They destroyed the Blacks, but they also destroyed themselves. That was my last sign, and then I knew all. I called upon the Browns, upon all the living dead in the world.

"In his lifetime, Shelk built a palisade of wood. I have built a palisade of Brown protectors. Thus it was ordained, and thus it must be done. I am Shelk's daughter and I carry out his will."

Avens turned her face to Whitespear, and he saw two vertical furrows on her brow. She is old, he thought in sudden fright, she is as old as Time itself. She is no longer my sister.

"Blood flows," said Avens with a shrug, "but it does not concern me. It is nothing compared with the horror of the living dead, the injustice of Blue Lake, the children unborn, the death of the innocent Whites. What I do is right."

"You kill," said Whitespear with a shudder. "You kill those who are innocent."

"They believe themselves to be innocent, and so their guilt is even greater in the eyes of Shelk."

"No!" cried Whitespear. "To kill is the greatest ill deed. Do you make a picture for the dead, Avens? Do you give them an afterlife? What do the Powers say?"

"You!" Avens mocked. "You say that, you who have set yourself up against the Powers."

"What does Helleborine say? Do you still remember him, Avens? He does not fail, he is a good man!"

"We are keeping vigil over Helleborine this very night." Avens rose and made Whitespear a sign to follow her.

The old healer lay on a bed of pine branches. His eyes were closed. Whitespear touched his face: it was icy. Within him arose images of the old man who cried out to another world.

And who spat in the face of a dead man.

"It is thawing," said Avens. "Tomorrow we shall dig his grave. Tomorrow we shall build his cairn."

"How did he die?" asked Whitespear fearfully. "By your hand?"

"He died in the fullness of his life. Look at him! You can see that he died in peace, beloved by us all. He was firm at my side, he read the purpose of the Powers. And you spoke of pictures for the dead, Whitespear: yes, I have made a picture for him. But you can do a better one."

She held out the piece of antler, and he saw the sign of Man on it. In sudden anger he struck it out of her hand and stormed:

"Then he, too, has turned traitor! You have bewitched them all. They serve the Destroyer in your name and in that of Shelk!"

"Yes," said Avens. "Marten and Gale, too."

Whitespear's anger ebbed away and all he felt was a deep sorrow. "You are in truth Shelk's daughter. No longer are you my sister."

He turned away, and during that night they kept vigil, unreconciled, over Helleborine's corpse.

.   .   .

In the blue light of early morning, Avens stood up. In a conciliatory tone, she said, "Your woman has been here, Whitespear."

Whitespear gave a shudder; the sleepless night was telling on him. Slowly, the meaning of her words dawned upon him. "Kite?" he asked.

"Kite, with her child and her servant. It was nearly a moon ago."

"Where is she now?"

"She went south, to Swidden Moor. She came here in search of Helleborine. He was very weak, but it gave him great happiness to see her. They spoke together for three days."

"But—how did she know? How did she find the way here?"

"Heather, her White servant, knew the way. He used to live here as a young man."

Whitespear nodded. Of course! He remembered Heather's tale.

"And how did you get here, Whitespear?" asked Avens.

"I followed Singletusk. We came from the north. And I'm the one who has a compact with him, not you, Avens."

Her face hardened. "That is not true. Singletusk has been here at Caribou Lake for the last two moon-quarters."

"Impossible! You don't know what you're talking about!"

"I should know. We feed him hay every day."

Whitespear shook his head. "I don't understand. I have tracked Singletusk from the north for two quarters and more."

"You have tracked a phantom, Whitespear. Singletusk is here, with me."

They were interrupted by a loud cry, followed by the sound of mammoths trumpeting. Avens rushed to the gate, with Whitespear at her heels. Outside there was a narrow strip of woods, and they ran through it and came to the edge of a wide glade. In it they saw two mammoths, standing eye to eye.

Both were immensely large, but the first thing they noticed about them was that each had lost one of its tusks. The way they were standing now, Avens and Whitespear viewed them from the side where the tusks were broken; the stumps were a couple of feet in length. Whitespear recognized one of the bulls, the one to the left: it was his Singletusk, his partner. The great left tusk shone white in the half-light of dawn. The other bull must be Avens's Singletusk: his right tusk was intact.

The two mammoth bulls were equals. They were standing a few feet apart, each measuring up the other one. It was an eerie sight; they were like an image and its counterimage in an invisible, vertical sheet of water. Which one was real, which one just a reflection? Whitespear remembered Centaury and her picture in the rock pool. Was the Healer nothing but the counterimage of the Destroyer? There they were, and they were determined, they wanted to find out. One of them was real: which one?

The trunks moved. For a moment they stretched out, almost meeting, as if in supplication. Then they turned down and rolled up in readiness for battle. The tusks, which seemed luminous in the rising light, arched majestically, their points turned inward. No eye could tell which was the bigger: they were image and counterimage.

All was still, as if frozen: the two great black shapes on the snow-patched ground, and behind them the dark forest, the dawn breaking over its edge.

As if by agreement, they both advanced a couple of steps, and a crack rang out when the tusks crossed. It was as though they had broken through the mirror and pushed their tusk-points into the water. They were still standing well apart, touching only with the extreme ends of their tusks. They strained, each testing the other one's strength. They respected each other; they knew themselves to be equals.

They made a few sparring movements, striking their tusks together repeatedly. They advanced another step, so that the tusks were crossed for their whole length, and again each tried to push the other to the side.

Finally they glided together as if drawn by an irresistible force, until the two tusk-stumps locked together. They started to trumpet wildly in an eruption of fury, terror, and pain. They tottered back and forth and turned slowly around, so that the uninjured tusks, which had been hidden from the spectators, came into view.

The tooth of Left Tusk was the longer. Its point had pierced Right Tusk's eye and buried itself deeply in the lacerated eye socket, from which a stream of blood coursed down the cheek. Right Tusk's tooth, which was two handsbreadths shorter, had bitten into the root of Left Tusk's trunk. There was a gush of blood each time the bull trumpeted. Thus the two stood locked in a death-grip. Whitespear, struck dumb, heard a shriek of horror from Avens.

Out of the forest bounded a grey shape, galloping, whimpering, yelping. It was a young wolf, thin, haggard, and hungry: he had smelled the blood. He began to dance around the fighting giants. In his agitated haste he tore straight into a big haystack, Avens's gift to Singletusk. The wolf made a somersault in a cloud of flying straws, got back on his legs, and continued his crazy capering.

The two bulls were trying desperately to disentangle themselves, but the tusks only bit deeper. Still they turned around and around, trampling in their own blood and the red-stained snow. The wolf ran from side to side, ready to bite, but not daring. Blood spouted from the trunk and mouth of Left Tusk; he was fighting for breath. Out of Right Tusk's terribly savaged eye socket flowed a steady stream of blood. No more were they able to express their suffering and terror. They were standing still now; they had surrendered; they were through. Avens sank to the ground, sobbing.

The bulls did not move.

The wolf slunk here and there, and his subdued yelps reached the spectators through the rush of the waterfall. He ventured ever closer; there was a glimpse of his teeth as he snapped at the legs of the mammoths.

The sun was up, moving in a low orbit above the edge of the forest. And still the giants were on their legs, drawing painful, heaving breaths.

Whitespear saw a woman emerge from the forest and walk across the glade. She looked at the mammoths, awed and fearful. Then she skirted them, came up to the small group of spectators, and bent over Avens. Gently she helped her up.

The wolf jumped up and bit Left Tusk in the foreleg.

The two mammoths tottered, with a deep sigh. Then they toppled over as a single block, on top of the wolf. There was a crunching sound as the bones in his body were broken, and the air was forced out of his lungs in a dreadful howl.

Left Tusk lay dead. Right Tusk's legs twitched a few times, then he too was still. The people, Avens, Whitespear, and the Brown protectors, stood as if paralyzed, staring at the enormous black bodies.

All except the Brown woman who had just arrived. She

turned to Avens and said urgently, "Avens, I wish to report on my journey."

In contrast to the other Browns, she spoke in the language of the Blacks. Avens looked at her vacantly, apparently not taking in her words.

"According to my mission," the woman resumed in a droning voice (she spoke deliberately and with a strong accent, but was clearly proud of her mastery of the language), "I went east to collect news from the Brown protectors, all the way to the coast. The tidings are good, Avens, except for one thing. Rowan is dead. I found him on my way out, a quarter from here, but according to my mission"—a phrase she seemed to be fond of—"I went on to the east."

"Rowan is dead," repeated Avens mechanically. "Yes, I see . . . How did it happen?"

"He was killed by a Black man," said the Brown woman, delighted with her news and its importance. "Before that, though, Rowan had killed a White woman. By mistake, I daresay—Rowan was always careless. But there is no cause for worry, Avens. According to my mission, I killed the Black man. So I took revenge for Rowan, although he wasn't worth much."

Avens made an effort to collect herself. "You killed the Black man . . ." she faltered.

"According to . . ." the woman began, but something in Avens's face made her check herself. "The Black man had a charm. I took care of it. Here it is." She pulled out an object from her birchbark carryall and handed it over.

Avens stared at it, her face turned ashen. It was the tiger tooth, the great tooth worn by Tiger. It glittered in her hand like the crescent moon.

She looked up and drew a few deep breaths. Then, in a clear strong voice, she called out:

"The compact has ended! Let the message go out to all the protectors! The compact has ended! Let everybody go back to their homes! *The compact has ended!*"

She turned to Whitespear and held out the tooth. He took it with shaking hands. Avens opened her mouth, her eyes sought his, but she was no longer able to speak. She tottered and would have fallen, had not Whitespear caught her in his arms. Thus they remained standing for a long time, Whitespear weeping silently, but Avens speechless, with open mouth.

And from that day, so it has been told, from that day and to the end of her long life, Avens never uttered another word.

ORIOLE

"And what happened to them?" asked Oriole. "Avens, Marten, and Gale, your half-brother and your half-sisters?"

"They went home, like all the others. They live on Veyde's Island, or so I have been told. I never went back."

"And the others? Kite, Wolf, your mother Hind?"

Whitespear smiled. "They live in Horn Lake Village. Kite is now the Shaman of Swidden Moor, for Harrier died three winters ago. Her fame has reached far and wide; she is the greatest shaman in the land. People from all around come to Swidden Moor to be healed by her. But I think that at least as many again come just to goggle at the Whites: Heather and his family. He remains a true servant to Kite—he could barely force himself to leave her long enough to go to the coast for his woman and child. And so Kite's fame grows ever greater: a shaman who has the Trolls in her service, so they say!

"I have made peace between Kite and me, and before he died, Harrier dubbed me a shaman, too. I look in at Swidden Moor now and then to be together with Kite and with our son Wolf, who is her apprentice. But Kite's rules are too strict for me, and so it came about that I joined Jay and became a traveler. It's a good life. I am a shaman, an artist, and a trader, and wherever I come I am a welcome guest.

"But now, Oriole, I want to know why you are here, and how you managed to find me. Tell me about yourself and about Siskin your mother."

"Siskin still lives in Oyster Village by the Salt Sea," Oriole told him. "When she arrived there, the old Chief, Diver, took such pleasure in her that he made her his woman, and to me he was like a father until he died, two winters ago.

"Even when I was a child I wanted to make pictures. Many of the old people were against it, as being unfitting for a girl. But old Diver, who loved me, was on my side. And my mother was pleased and proud, and she told me about you and of her great love for you. So I was apprenticed to the artist of Oyster Village. But my mother always wanted me to be taught by you when I grew up."

Whitespear looked at her thoughtfully. "Can you show me something?" he asked.

The girl timidly produced a piece of antler on which she had engraved a bison. Whitespear studied the picture and nodded. "Yes, you have the gift," he said. "It isn't quite right here—and there—but it lives. You have the gift."

Oriole lit up and went on breathlessly: "Last summer my uncle Hedgehog from Falcon Hill came to us in Oyster Village. He wanted to tell my mother of their father's death."

"Yes," said Whitespear, "Otter was killed by a bison. He died a brave man's death, saving Heather's life. At that time Kite wanted me to become Chief in Otter's stead, but I did not agree: that she finds it hard to forgive."

"Anyway, Hedgehog told us you were a frequent visitor at Falcon Hill. And so, when he returned home, I went along with him. And my being here now is by my mother's wish as much as my own.

"When we came to Falcon Hill they told us that you had been there and left only a couple of days before. It was easy to track you in the snow. And we found the place where you'd been attacked."

"Yes, I'm a lone walker now, since Jay died. Two ruffians ambushed me, struck me down, and took all my things. Alas, Jay was right: if you carry treasure, you should not walk alone. Still, I have my life, and I can make new treasures."

"The evildoers will be caught. Hedgehog sent his hunters to track them down. You will get your treasures back, Father."

They laughed, and Whitespear sat up. "And now, thanks to your help and the food you brought, I'm ready to go with you to Falcon Hill."

"Are you ready to go with me to Oyster Village too, Father?"

Whitespear pulled at his beard. "What does your mother say about that?"

"It is her greatest wish. Do come! Siskin is still the fairest woman on the shores of the Salt Sea, and she wants to have a love-child with you."

Whitespear pulled out a pouch from underneath his blouse. Out of it he took four things. The first was the big flat tiger tooth, the second a firestone, the third a piece of flint. The fourth was a peculiar oblong, rounded stone.

"The robbers didn't find my greatest treasures," he said. "I have the tooth from Tiger my father, and he had it from his father. But the thunderbolt was given to me by Jay when he lay dying. It has helped me once, maybe it will again."

"He gave you his most precious possession!" Oriole marveled. "Didn't he want it to go to his son?"

"I offered to carry it to his sons in Birchneck Village. But he laughed, though he was in pain, and said, 'In the Land of Flints the thunderbolts lie about on the ground. All you need to do is stoop down for them.' 'But you found this one in a tree,' I reminded him. He gave me a wink and said, 'Oh yes, I'd forgotten. Don't you forget it, now.' "

Whitespear heaved himself up and stood on his legs. With his arm around his daughter's shoulders he stepped out of the little tent that Hedgehog had made for him. They could hear the ravens calling, and suddenly a rutting fox gave a terrific yell. Whitespear drew breath deeply. "That's the sign," he said. "Spring is coming."

.   .   .

The Browns, my Oriole, are guests in the world of men. They are in it for a short time. They carry all of man's suffering and none of his hope. Then they are gone.

Thus Whitespear might have spoken, and he might have continued:

One of them remains. That is Shelk. He waxes ever greater. Already his name is too holy to be mentioned; he acquires new names—the Morning Star, the Evening Star, the Guardian of Birds. Soon he will be the builder of the sky's vault, the maker of stars and suns, the ruler of winds and waves, the One who blew a living spirit into men and animals. Then he will be the Supreme Guardian.

And the sons and daughters of the Sonless One will fall down in worship before his face.

 **POSTSCRIPT**

The life of early man, we are told, was brief, brutish, and bestial. Yet the fossil evidence suggests a very different picture, at any rate for the last 50,000 years or so of the Ice Age. (The total duration of the Ice Age was 1.5 million years, but here we are concerned only with its final part.) The truth is that Ice Age man in Europe was longer-lived and better nourished than his successors up to recent times. Only in the last century or so has a fraction of humanity attained a point where the demography of the late Ice Age is surpassed. As for brutality, the weapons of Ice Age man were used for hunting, which at least in European latitudes was the main livelihood, and evidence for warlike aggression is sparse and uncertain. As for bestiality, Ice Age man had remarkable cultural capacity, and some of the preserved works are among the finest ever created.

The Neandertals existed in Europe for at least 100,000 years, and they form the climax of a European evolutionary lineage that started perhaps a million years earlier. During such a long time, and over an entire continent, we may suspect that a great variety of communities flourished, including some that would elicit our admiration and some that would seem detestable to us. I have chosen to present a congenial Neandertal community because that makes the story more interesting, but there are additional reasons. Some early Neandertals were cannibals, such as those of Krapina in Yugoslavia around 100,000 years ago, but later Neandertals buried their dead—sometimes on a bed of flowers, like those found in Shanidar Cave in Iraq. Furthermore, they were long-lived and took good care of their old and incapacitated.

Apparently Neandertal man's successors in Europe, the so-called Cro-Magnons *(Homo sapiens)*, were not particularly warlike either. They have left thousands of pictures for posterity, and these show the things that were important in their lives. Look at the pictures of Babylon, Assyria, Egypt, all the great civilizations: endless processions of warriors, hecatombs of vanquished enemies; the victorious king-hero trampling his foes underfoot and receiving obsequious homage. The art of the Ice Age moves in a different sphere altogether, the subjects being animals, plants, hunters, women, erotic activity. There are heroes, too, but the adversary that they meet and that may kill them is the big game animal: in a famous scene from Lascaux, the hunter falls victim to a wounded bison. Again (and I owe this observation to Carl-Axel Moberg), the weapons in the archaeological material are those of the hunter, such as the spear and the harpoon, and not those of the warrior, the sword and shield and mace. And so we may conclude that wars are by no means "natural" to man. This is in contrast to the tenets of what is called social Darwinism—a silly misnomer, incidentally, since Darwin himself viewed it with great mistrust.

Clearly both these peoples were something other, and

something much more interesting, than the grunting cave-
men of the popular imagination—different, too, from Rous-
seau's virtuous savage. In currently fashionable myths, early
man has been depicted as a killer ape, or as an inoffensive
gatherer of shellfish—to mention just two alternatives.
Whatever grain of truth there may be in such suggestions
relates to a much earlier stage of human evolution. The people of the later Ice Age were definitely human beings, and
we may expect to find in them the entire spectrum of humanity, from the fool to the sage and from the rascal to the
saint. They lived within the constraints of their environment
and of their own beliefs and customs, yet they were forever
pushing at those constraints, looking for shortcuts to happiness. Love and hate, daring and cowardice, vanity and hu-
mility, strength and weakness: it was all there, for these
people were our own flesh and blood.

One of my special targets is the Alley Oop figure of Neandertal man with his shambling walk, awkward movements,
and general bestiality. It originated with early paleontologists who saw what they wanted to see—a creature recently
risen from the apes, one that made a pleasing contrast with
our own superiority. We now know that the chronology of
human evolution goes back much farther and that early man
was a perfect biped almost 4 million years ago, as proved by
fossil footprints. Thus, Pleistocene man presumably moved
with the grace and precision of a highly trained athlete.

These were some of the things I attempted to tell in *Dance
of the Tiger*. Yet much remained to be told about Ice Age
man: hence the present book.

When you try to visualize a world at a distance of 30,000
years, from which no voices in the form of written words
can reach us, you have to rely on three things: facts, speculation based on facts, and imagination. The class of facts, in
this case, comprises not only the archaeological and paleon-
tological finds as such but also their scientific interpretation,

and indeed, the results of Ice Age research in general. We do, for instance, know a great deal about the climatic history of the Ice Age: about the plants and animals which then existed in Europe; about the body build and habits of Neandertal man (for example, that he used to squat on his heels). Within the class of speculation falls the thesis that the people of the late Ice Age in Europe were, on the whole, kindly and non-aggressive. Finally, when the Neandertals are pictured as matriarchal and the hybrids as sterile, this is pure imagination.

A brief survey of the scientific background *Singletusk* draws on seems called for here. The story takes place towards the end of a warmer climatic phase, the so-called Denekamp interstadial, which occurred about 30,000 years ago and was succeeded by the last great advance of the ice. As in *Dance of the Tiger,* the relationships between the Neandertals—the "Whites"—the aboriginal men of Europe, and the recently immigrant "Blacks," or modern *Homo sapiens,* play an important part. It now appears that Neandertals and sapiens coexisted in Europe for some time, perhaps a thousand years or more.

In this story, the Neandertals are depicted as light-complexioned, and there is good evidence for this. Neandertal bone structure is extraordinarily dense, which proves that they had an excellent supply of vitamin D. European winters (at least north of the Alps) are poor in sunlight, and a dark-pigmented skin might easily be the cause of vitamin D deficiency, with resulting brittleness of bone, or osteoporosis. A strong selection pressure for loss of pigment may be deduced.

The invading sapiens, who apparently entered Europe from the south, are pictured here as brown-skinned and black-haired. The same type of selection would presumably come into play to bring about a subsequent loss of pigment.

It is generally assumed that Ice Age men lived in small groups of twenty-five to thirty people, rather widely scattered but with brisk intergroup contacts. The density of the population may have been on the order of 1 individual to 25 square kilometers (about 10 square miles). The average distance between settlements would then be 20 to 30 kilometers (12 to 19 miles). Their existence was largely dependent on the so-called Mammoth Steppe, which covered great parts of Europe during the cold spells and was restricted to the north (northern Scandinavia, for example) during the warmer phases. The immense productivity of the Mammoth Steppe would spill over into neighboring areas during the seasonal migration of the game, bringing mammoth, reindeer, and other northern species into the forested areas farther south for the winter. In the summer, other kinds of game, such as bison, horse, and several species of deer, would be available, as well as fish in the lakes and streams and a great variety of plant foods.

We know nothing about the language of these Ice Age people. Their highly organized culture and their anatomy (which, as far as the sapiens are concerned, was identical with our own) suggest that their language was as fully structured and expressive as that of any present-day hunting peoples. For this reason, it should be rendered as a timeless "modern" language (they, of course, spoke the modern language of their time). To do otherwise would be to defer to an unconscious racism that tries to make our early forerunners seem distant, odd, and even dimwitted.

In the notes that follow I discuss other speculations I have made based on fact, and deal with some points that may have seemed surprising or obscure.

Neandertals · and · Sapiens

At the time *Dance of the Tiger* was written, the coexistence of Neandertals and sapiens (Cro-Magnons) in Europe was regarded by many students as probable but not proven. New evidence tends to bear out the probability. At Saint-Césaire in France a Neandertal burial was found in association with the Châtelperronian culture, dated as flourishing between 34,000 and 31,000 BP (before present), indicating that Neandertals were still extant at the latter date. On the other hand, anatomically modern men, or sapients, of the Combe-Capelle and Cro-Magnon strains (which, on the whole, are just modern Europeans) are associated with the Aurignacian culture, beginning at least 32,000 BP. The oldest find of a sapient in Europe (from Kelsterbach in Germany) is dated at 31,200 BP. There are also sites where an alternation of Châtelperronian and Aurignacian cultures has been reported, which might mean that the two types of men alternated in possession. On this reading of the evidence, they coexisted in Europe for a fairly long time, perhaps a thousand years or more. (Other readings are possible and may eventually prove to be correct, but at present the evidence favors this one. At the time of writing, the material from Saint-Césaire has not been published in detail, so we mustn't be dogmatic.) Whether such was the case or not, the Neandertals nevertheless vanished without leaving any anatomical impress on the sapients. This strengthens the idea of two species reproductively isolated from each other. In the model I use here, the isolation was due to infertility of the species hybrids, but other models are certainly possible (I can easily think of several) and perhaps more probable.

The most interesting thing about the Châtelperron-Neandertal constellation is that the Châtelperronian is an advanced culture of the Upper Paleolithic type, rich in tool forms and featuring elegant flint blades that were struck off by means of bone or antler punches instead of the stone hammers of the Mousterian culture, which in Europe is undoubtedly Neandertal. For this reason the Châtelperronian was held to be the work of modern *Homo sapiens,* as is true of the Aurignacian and later Upper Paleolithic cultures. On the other hand, there is evidence that the Châtelperronian evolved out of the Mousterian, and so it should not be too surprising to find that Neandertals were its authors—as soon as we discard the idea that they were incapable of making important cultural innovations.

It is now evident that *Homo sapiens* and *Homo neanderthalensis* represent two distinct evolutionary lineages, although there are a few diehard opponents to this view. In recent years, sapiens have been traced back 100,000 years and even more in Africa, so it must be assumed that the two lineages diverged from each other well before that date. The two species are similar in some respects: they have larger brains than their predecessors and both developed advanced cultures. (This is called parallel evolution, and is very common in the fossil record.) In most anatomical features, on the other hand, they are dissimilar—the result of divergent evolution. Exactly when the two lineages split up is not known. That event could even date back to between 0.7 and 1 million years BP, when the ancestors of the Neandertals first entered Europe.

Stars · and · Constellations

The positions of the stars change over the millennia for two reasons: their own proper motions and the precession of the equinoxes. The latter results in the north celestial pole moving in a circle (many thousand years ago, for instance, Vega took the position of North Star), returning to the same position in 26,000 years. Thirty thousand years ago, the present-day Stella Polaris was quite close to the celestial pole, and, as the fixed pivot of the night sky, doubtless was used for orientation. (We know that many ancient cultures regarded the North Star as the most important star and an object of worship, though the North Pole as such was unknown to them.)

The proper motions of the stars may lead to distinct

changes in the constellations even in such a comparatively short time as 30,000 years. The changes can be calculated, as Dr. Göran Sandell has kindly done for the two prominent northern constellations, the Big Dipper (Great Bear) and Cassiopeia. As shown in the accompanying picture, the Dipper did not differ much from its present shape (it is the Great Swan of the Whites and the Mammoth of the Blacks). Cassiopeia, on the other hand, looked very different from the big W now to be seen in the sky. Note especially that three brilliant stars (left to right, Delta, Gamma, and Beta) were then practically in a straight line, which must have been the constellation's most striking characteristic. (Delta and Gamma Cassiopeiae were much closer together than now, separated by an arc of little more than one degree.) They formed a triangle with the even brighter Alpha (bottom of picture). The less brilliant star Epsilon, which now forms the left leg of the W, would then have appeared more isolated, and might not always have been considered part of the constellation. In the story, this constellation is the Long-Tailed Duck of the Whites (Epsilon being the tail) and the Mammoth Spear of the Blacks (the triangle forming the spearpoint).

The · Smoke · Offering

It may be superfluous to explain the smoke offering gone wrong in the "Baywillow" chapter, the phenomenon being very common. If the ground is cold, an inversion may develop in the air layers just above it—that is to say, the temperature will rise with increased elevation instead of falling as is normal. Rising smoke will tend to be arrested between the two gradients, which is why we are likely to get a pall of smog over large cities on clear, cold winter days. (Cain didn't know this.)

The Big Dipper, or Great Bear, 30,000 years ago

Cassiopeia, 30,000 years ago
(shown at twice the scale of the Dipper)

The · Black · Wine

The art of making fermented beverages is common to almost all vigorous cultures, though the raw materials may vary widely—milk, grapes, rice, berries, sap, honey. "Wine," to most of us, means wine made from grapes, which of course were not at hand there and then. I have been unfairly castigated for having my Cro-Magnons (or Blacks) make wine, for the drink made from berries is also styled wine. Although the sugar content of berries is too low to produce a strong wine, it can be supplemented by adding honey (rare, from wild bees), sap (plentiful), or other plant juices. For instance, the sugary pith of the rosebay (*Epilobium,* also called fireweed) was used for this purpose in Kamchatka.

As to the merits of the product, it should be remembered that northern berries, which ripen during the long summer days, are much superior to any southern fruits in the quality and intensity of their flavor. (The same holds true for cultivated berries: just compare a Scandinavian strawberry with the insipid variety harvested farther south.) Even a crude product will retain some of the excellence of the raw material.

A great deal of lore and superstition would naturally have grown up around the mysterious process of fermentation—for instance, about the fact that *Vaccinium* berries such as the bilberry or lingonberry will not ferment by themselves (see the chapter "Hind"). Rowan berries, on the other hand, do so readily, with the result that waxwings and other birds feeding on them may get sadly drunk (see "Kite").

The · Thunderbolt

The "thunderbolt" that plays an important suggestive role in the chapter "Jay" is a belemnite, a fossil relative of today's cuttlefish and squids, which is very common in the chalk of southern Sweden (the Land of Flints). Sometimes called a thunderstone, it is a massive calcareous rod with a conspicuously phallic shape, and so has been important in popular belief. (A more flippant appellation is "the Devil's cigar.") The connection with thunder and lightning is not far-fetched: a heavy rain will often lay bare many specimens. The story of the "tree-bolt" is, of course, an unabashed lie.

The · Fight · of · the · Mammoths

The fight between the mammoths that kill each other because both have lost one of their tusks sounds like a particularly tall story. Nonetheless, it is perfectly true, although in reality it happened elsewhere and at another time. The material has not yet been published, and so I cannot go into details, but I can assure the reader that the account is based on careful study of the find and that the whole thing must have happened, by and large, in the way described in the chapter "Singletusk." This is true, too, for the hapless wolf flattened beneath the toppling mammoths (it was actually a coyote).

If the skull of a mammoth is viewed from above, the tusks form an elegant lyrate shape with the points turning inward. (Many mammoth pictures that we see are incorrect because the position of the left and right tusks has been reversed!) Thus the bulls could engage in ritual fights without causing serious damage. However, should one of the tusks be broken, the other would automatically become a lethal weapon. If both bulls had a broken tusk, they would slip inside each other's guard and be locked in a deadly grip.

ABOUT · THE · AUTHOR

Björn Kurtén was born in Finland in 1924. A professor at the University of Helsinki and one of Europe's leading paleontologists, he has worked extensively in Europe, Africa, and North America. Professor Kurtén has published several novels in Swedish and numerous books in English on mammals and the ice ages, among them *Dance of the Tiger, The Cave Bear Story, Not from the Apes,* and *The Ice Age.* He is a fellow of the Explorers Club and has held a lectureship in zoology at Harvard University.